Papaya Tree

ORCHID BLOOM

Paperback ISBN: 978-988-79891-2-7

Written by Orchid Bloom
Published by S.Y. Johnson
Cover art by Sabina Kencana
Edited by Glenys Dreyer
Publishing Assistant Victoria Dreyer

Translated and published in English with permission.

First Edition

To Sally Bunker, the 'young lady,'
whose eyes sparkle
whenever she talks about her botanical art;
who has inspired me that
it's never too late to start a second career;
whose spider reminds us not to forget
to pause every now and then
to notice the beauties around us.

Author's Notes

Orchid: Do you think it's a privilege to be born as a boy in an indigenous village?

Villager: Ha-ha, to a degree, yes. Although in recent years, village people also pass on their wealth to girls. In the past, they would rather pass onto nephews and brothers to keep the wealth within the family of the same last name.

Orchid: Do think you boys are even more treasured these days over girls as the property prices rise?

Villager: Probably, it only concerns those families who still own lots of land. Nevertheless, boys are always treasured more than girls in our tradition. But not because of the rise in property price.

Orchid: Please tell me more about that.

Villager: Only a boy's name can go onto the family book. Without a male descendant, the lineage cannot be continued. Soon your family will lose your household register. That, probably is one of the most important things to the indigenous villagers, to carry on the bloodline.

Orchid: What do you think of the value of 'Ding' rights these days?

Villager: In the past, many uneducated villagers struggled to make ends meet. They had no savings to build houses. Back then, the village houses were not worth as much as they are today, so many of them sold their 'Ding' rights for quick money. However, in recent years, the Hong Kong Government has tightened the rule, and as results, no 'Ding' rights can be transferred. You can be put into jail for trading the 'Ding' rights. As far as I know, no one is willing to take the risk anymore. Therefore, it's still the same thing - the 'Ding' is worth nothing unless you have pieces of land.

Orchid: What do you think would be the future of the 'Small House Policy'?

Villager: The policy will end when the indigenous people run out of the land that their ancestors owned, it's as simple as that.

Orchid: You think that the policy only benefits the big land-owners these days as the 'Ding' only has its worth if one has a piece of land?

Villager: Of course, it's been the case and always will be; the poor remain poor, and the rich get richer.

I live in one of the indigenous villages in Hong Kong. The peace, calmness, and beauties of nature here inspire me. The only things I experience from my interactions with the indigenous people are kindness, generosity, and great hospitality. As an outsider, I was envious of the privileges the indigenous male descendants could enjoy - to be able to build a house on land granted to him when he turns eighteen, a house that nowadays is worth millions of dollars. Since only boys could enjoy their 'Ding' rights, that raised the question of how they valued girls in the grand scheme of things.

However, as I wrote the story and understood more about the history and the dynamics, I came to realise that it was not as simple as I thought. The indigenous people are one very tight unit. This unit is confined and restricted by many traditions and values that have been passed on for generations, and still remained very strong among them - in which the values of family, obligation, integrity, and interdependency are essentials to the survival and flourish of their groups.

'Papaya Tree' is a work of pure fiction. All the characters and plots were written entirely out of my wild imagination. No mention of names or developments should be associated with any real-life objects or establishments. No regulations or policies mentioned are to be taken as facts. I have done my research on the Small House Policy, as well as asked questions to indigenous residents on their views regarding certain subjects, including the interview recorded above. I am deeply grateful for their selfless contribution to 'Papaya Tree.' If there is any inaccuracy or confusions in any parts of the story, the faults and mistakes are solely and entirely mine.

'Ding Rights'

In 1972, the British government introduced the Small House Policy in Hong Kong. The policy allows each indigenous male villager who is descended from the male lineage of a resident in a village (Ding) at the time of 1898*, one concession to build a small house, a standard, stand-alone; a three-storey house of seven hundred square feet in size on each floor, in his lifetime. The policy served the purpose at the time to help the colonial government to gain support to develop the New Territories in order to meet the increasing housing demand, as well as to prevent another riot resembling that in 1967. After the handover of Hong Kong's sovereignty to China, the Policy remained protected by Article 40 under the Basic Law. The Chinese government pledged to respect the traditions and the indigenous people's right to their ancestral lands.

In recent years, there have been more controversies over gender inequality, since female descendants are not entitled to any Ding rights, as well as that between indigenous villagers and the general public as a whole, as the city is getting more crowded and the demand in housing is getting acute. The rise of property prices also puts the citizens who are born with Ding rights to an unfair advantage over the rest of the population.

* June 9, 1898, was the year when the Qing China and the United Kingdom signed a convention to extend the Hong Kong territory to include today's Kowloon and the New Territories.

CHAPTER ONE

Jessica took a last long drag from her cigarette before extinguishing it in the ashtray she hid in the garden. She had to beat the mosquitoes and go inside the house before they came out to hunt at sunset. She picked up her weekend bag and walked around the back of the house - she wanted to stop by and check on the papaya tree.

"Ooh, hello, little one." Jessica was delighted to find a new small papaya tree branching out from its mother trunk. The papaya tree in the back garden of her family house had just begun to grow when she left Hong Kong for London more than three years ago. This papaya tree had never ceased to fascinate her ever since. Every time she came back, she discovered some new development. Over the past few years, the papaya tree had grown from a small bush to a handsome, tall tree. It also gave birth to six small papaya trees that branched out from it like a second-tier on a Christmas tree.

She found the tree a perfect symbol of her family as she had five siblings. Her third sister, Janice, recently gave birth to her first child, George. The new baby tree budding from a lower level made a timely appearance to mark a new generation. A papaya tree usually had a lifespan of four to five years, but she suspected this one was going to last for a very long time, given the new trees it kept giving birth to.

No one else in her family seemed to pay much attention to this special papaya tree, mainly due to the abundance of them in the village. They were everywhere. Every house in the village had at least one to two papaya trees. When one died, there was always another one, or more, that budded somewhere else to replace it. The birds which fed on the papaya kept the species alive in the village by spreading its seeds everywhere.

It only took months for its fruit to ripen, so the villagers never ran out of papaya. The papaya had integrated into part of the villagers' diet since many generations ago. Besides consuming it on its own as fruit and juice, papaya salad, papaya stir fry, papaya cake, and papaya soup were the villagers' favourite household dishes. Papaya soup was particularly highly regarded for its effectiveness in bringing in milk for nursing mothers.

Thinking of nursing, Jessica wondered if Janice was still breastfeeding George, as she remembered her sister told her how much she was struggling with it the last time when she was here.

George's grandfather passed away a couple of weeks ago, and Jessica's parents insisted that she must come back to attend the funeral. Her sister's father-in-law was hardly a close relative but given how big and important her brother-in-law's family was, and the fact that her sister was married to the eldest son - the first heir - her mother insisted that the whole family should be at the funeral to pay respect to the late paternal grandfather of her first grandchild. Like everything else in the family, most decisions were made based on someone's hierarchy in the family or in the village. Credits, capabilities, and feelings were only secondary factors.

Jessica stepped into the house and saw his brother, Joe, playing video games with his feet up on the coffee table. He turned his head slightly and spotted Jessica's entrance.

"Bring me a bottle of beer from the fridge, sis." Joe gave her the order without even saying hello. Jessica ignored him and headed upstairs to her room. Behind her back, she heard Joe shout, "Beer, NOW!" followed by the hurrying footsteps of her mother.

Jessica paused. She carried on after listening to the sound of a bottle landing on the table, then the noise of the battle gunshots from the video game filled the living room again.

Jessica quickly unpacked her bag and hung everything up in her wardrobe. She collapsed onto her bed, suddenly feeling exhausted. She could hardly sleep on the plane. Flying long haul in coach was no luxury.

Although her father generously paid for the plane ticket every time she was summoned home for a family occasion, she reminded herself that all males in the family flew in business class whenever they travelled. Her mother's tolerance to Joe's behaviour reminded her once again that she'd made the right decision to accept the scholarship from the Society of Botanical Artist in the U.K. to study botanical art history abroad. In return, she had to research and write a thesis on that in the Far East on the organisation's credits.

Her frequent sponsored trips back in Hong Kong allowed her to make savings on her budget while carrying out her research after fulfilling whatever family obligation the trip was for. She often stayed longer than she was asked by her parents. Over time, her family had little to complain about her leaving the nest as they saw her all the time.

"Jessica!" Her mothers summon had drawn her from her daydream back to reality. "Come down and help me set up the table for dinner!"

It didn't matter that Jessica had just got off the plane from a twelve-hour flight and she badly needed a shower - a daughter was expected to help out around the house, while a male family member was not required to lift a finger the moment he stepped into his home. They were the royalties in their own castle.

Dinner went uneventfully. Her father, Jaguar, walked into the house after everyone was seated at the dining table. No one dared to touch any food before their father joined the table, except Joe, snacking on some nuts that their mother, Helen, specially prepared for him.

Looking at the table, Jessica saw that her mother had prepared all the dishes favoured by her father, Joe, and her little brother Jay. Again, she laughed at herself for being naive enough to think, or hope, that her mother would prepare a dish or two that she knew she liked to show appreciation for the effort she'd made to fly all the way back to attend the funeral of Janice's father-in-law.

Jaguar and Joe dominated the conversations at the table. To them, none of the opinions of the rest of the family mattered.

These days, Jay also kept quiet - he was now regarded more or less like a woman after he'd bravely stepped out of the closet and announced that he was gay. Jessica loved her baby brother to bits. She always made sure to take time off and take the Eurostar to Paris to see Jay whenever he was there for work. Jay was an assistant designer for a French fashion brand. He worked in their Hong Kong office and helped the brand to develop the Asian line out of the brand's core collection every season. Jay loved his job and the chance to escape from the family saga a handful of times throughout the year to work in his beloved city of the French capital.

After dinner, she helped Janice to carry George to give her a break while they stepped out of the house to catch up in the garden before Janice had to head back to her in-laws' house.

"I can't imagine how you could live with your mother-in-law. And you look more tired than me, given that I've not slept in the last twenty hours. Why don't you hire a nanny to look after George at home? It's not that Paul can't afford it." Jessica noticed the black sacs below her sister's eyes. She had also lost all her pregnancy fat during the past few months while she was away. *Motherhood must be tough*, Jessica thought.

"Let's hope she won't be around for much longer now her husband is dead. And let others care for my son? No way. He is the first grandson of the first son of Lee's family. I can't afford to have him get hurt by anyone. No, I have to take care of him myself. He's just too precious."

"He is precious because he is your baby," Jessica argued.

"Of course, you know what I mean. I am lucky to have given birth to a boy. Look at Mabel, that poor thing. She is still talking about going for the fourth after giving birth to three girls. Three girls! She is going to be a pig after she is done with getting pregnant! I just managed to get rid of all my baby fat. I need to get Paul back into my bed, not in his mistress's, so that he can make me pregnant again with another boy." With that, Janice checked her tummy to make sure it did not bulge after dinner.

"First of all, our own mother went through the same thing. She had four of us girls before Joe was born. She looks nothing like a pig to me. Secondly, what are you talking about? Does Paul cheat on you?" Jessica felt her heart boiling for her sister. She and Janice had been close from childhood.

She found her two eldest sisters too serious to have any fun with. Jacqueline, the eldest, was a lawyer. Her mission was to protect her immediate and extended families' interests and fortunes. The second sister, Joanne, followed her parents' advice and studied to be an accountant. She served as the family accountant these days. Janice was only two years older than her, and she'd loved following her around since they were little girls. Janice was full of mischief and would take Jessica with her everywhere when she played pranks on different villagers. Janice was smart enough to tag Jessica along as even if they got into trouble, her parents would only punish them lightly because of Jessica. Her parents saw Jessica as their lucky charm as her mother fell pregnant with their baby brother, Joe, pretty much right after Jessica was born.

"Every man cheats, especially rich ones like my husband." Janice was not as diligent as her two older sisters. Her lack of diligence was compensated by her wittiness. She'd decided to become a real estate agent. She made much more money from the commissions she made from selling and letting properties than her two sisters did, who worked for the family and were paid only an allowance from the family trust. The transactions from the village houses she knew were alone sufficient to keep her busy and her bank account fat. The intel she gathered from her employment made her the most knowledgeable person when it came to who owned what.

Nevertheless, that was not enough for the ambitious Janice. She swore not to let the sons monopolise the fortune left to them by their ancestors. She believed if she could not beat the game, then she would join it and changed the rules from within. Ever since she was a teenager, she learned all the tricks on how to make herself look pretty and behave desirably. Men wanted to have her while women wanted to be her.

In the end, Janice successfully seduced the eldest son of the most powerful and wealthiest Lee clan, whose village was located merely twenty minutes by car from her own, the Ma's. Paul and Janice got married a bit more than a year ago and eleven months later, the first grandson of the new generation of the Lee clan, George, was born.

"How can you even let him touch you after he slept with another woman?" Jessica questioned her sister without believing what she just heard.

"Don't worry, I am going to make him pay for his sins one day. But for now, he is still useful to me. I need his seeds to produce more babies like this gorgeous boy." Janice bent down and planted a kiss on George's cheeks.

"Did you hear how you talked? Do you even love him?" Jessica was shocked by the icy tone in her sister's voice.

"My little sister, love comes in many forms. For now, I love the wealth and power Paul brings me. Although I won't be like mum, to hide and enslave myself in the kitchen for the rest of my life. And I won't allow George to become another Joe. He and my other sons will use the family's fortune and build another empire in the city; where there is no stupid indigenous law to govern how inheritance has to be passed down the lineage; where women, both mothers and daughters, can share the fruits of the profit."

Jessica had always admired her sister's determination, and she had no doubt Janice was going to succeed in what her sister told her she would do.

CHAPTER TWO

The next morning, Jessica went to see her grandfather. Her grandparents' house was only down the road from her parents. Her grandparents used to live in the traditional house that her parents, younger brothers, and her sister, Joanne, who was a spinster, lived in now. As her father, Jaguar, was the eldest son, he took over the family house after he got married to her mother, Helen.

The traditional Ma's house was vast in size. There were eight bedrooms spread across the upper floor of the house. The living room, dining room, kitchen, and a couple of guest rooms were on the ground level. There was a small building detached from the main house, which was used as the servant quarter. Back in the old days when Jaguar was a little boy, the house bustled with Chinese amahs who looked after the little ones and did all the housekeeping, cooking for Jessica's grandparents. These days as local labour costed a lot more, Jessica's parents hired a couple from the Philippines to work as the helper and gardener to help Helen around the house.

Her grandparents moved into a smaller but more modern house which was set up to be age-friendly. There was an elevator large enough for a wheelchair to be pushed in and out in the middle of the house for her grandparents to go up and down the house when it was needed one day. Though Jessica thought it would be a long time before her grandfather, Jackson, needed it.

She watched her grandfather from afar, admiring how handsome, elegant, and agile he still was in his seventies. One of Jackson's morning routine was to clear the weeds that grew near his house. He religiously did that to his own house and his three son's houses. He believed such a habit would save their properties and lives one day in the unfortunate case of fire. The memory of house fires back in his childhood's day remained fresh in his mind so that Jackson was on constant guard for anything that could easily catch fire.

"Grandpapa, I'm back," Jessica tiptoed to Jackson and whispered in his ears. Jackson nearly fell backwards and landed his bottom onto the ground. He quickly found his balance, stood up, padded the grass off his trousers, and pulled Jessica into an embrace.

"Jessica, what a lovely surprise! Although, one day you are going to give your grandpapa a heart attack."

"You are not going to have a heart attack, Grandpapa. Look at you! Vibrant and handsome as always. A gentleman like you has too big a heart to fail."

Jessica was right, her grandfather was an elegant, well-groomed old man. Even picking up grass in his garden, he dressed in his tailor-made suit and with a trilby on his head. Jackson grew up during the prime of the colonial days of the British rule. His family sent him to boarding school in England from a young age. Jessica's great grandparents had high hopes for their son to come back to the city and serve in the colonial government, to represent and fight for the rights of the indigenous clan. However, Jackson had little interest in politics. He chose to read English Literature and majored in Art at University. His passion for painting earned him a nickname of 'Village Picasso' among Ma's clan.

Jessica had inherited her grandfather's talent in drawing. When she was not playing with Janice or once Janice was old enough to ditch her to chase after boys, Jessica followed her grandpapa everywhere he went. He taught her all he knew in art as well as gardening. Jessica would not mind getting her hands dirty and helped her grandfather plant vegetables in the garden, caring for the trees and plants around the village. When the light was perfect, Jackson would suddenly announce to Jessica that they should paint. Jackson loved teaching Jessica about plants while painting them. Without knowing, Jessica unconsciously absorbed both skills like a sponge, examining the botanical part of a plant and drawing it in depth, and became the talented and trained botanical artist she was today.

Jessica's little tolerance to her brother Joe's behaviours, was also the result of growing up seeing how courteous her grandfather was with the others, especially ladies. Jackson always held the door for the ladies and stood up when a lady left the room. He had an impeccable hat etiquette. While her grandpapa annoyed the men in the village, the women were all charmed by his manners and charisma. Jessica knew very well why her grandpapa made a woman feel like a lady instead of a servant.

"What are you doing back here so soon? Did somebody die?" Jackson tried to recall from his memory if anyone he knew did not seem to be around for much longer.

"Yes! But not in our village. Janice's father-in-law, Patrick Lee, passed away. Mum made me come back for his funeral. Seriously, I had only met him once at Janice's wedding."

"Patrick Lee! I thought he was too arrogant to grow old. Popcorn time to see how his mistresses and bastard children fight over his fortune?" Jackson chuckled as he pictured the larger-than-life Patrick Lee.

"Grandpapa, you are so mean!" Jessica poked her grandfather's chest gently and joined him in picking up weeds. She loved spending time with her grandpapa as he was the only one in the family who was interested in and understood what she was doing in her work. She often picked his brain when she came across a tree or a plant that she was not familiar with. Or at times, when she had to go back to a tree's habitat to record its growth, Jackson would always be delighted to be her chaperone as she would need to hang out in a forest by herself for hours at a time.

Jessica enjoyed the stories Jackson shared with her about the good old days when he studied in the U.K. Ever since Jessica studied abroad, Jackson only spoke to her in English. He missed the English banter, and few people in the village could understand his posh English accent, and none could grasp his English jokes. He finally found the ears in his favourite grandchild.

"Do you have any mistresses hidden away? Uncles and aunts that I have never met?" Jessica suddenly wondered if her charming grandfather had ever been unfaithful to his wife.

"Me? I am too afraid of your grandma not giving me any pocket money or letting me keep my sports cars." Jackson grimaced at the mere thought of that. It was true that Jackson had never been interested in managing his own money. He had given his wife, Rose, the power to manage the family finance until their sons started their own families. Until today, Jackson relied on his wife to give him his weekly allowance. Jackson lived a rather simple life.

His only weak spots were tailor-made suits and sports cars. He named his first son, Jessica's father, after the sports car brand of which he had a few vintage models in the garage.

***

Jessica left Jackson reluctantly after lunch, as she promised Janice to help babysit George. Her grandmother Rose cooked her favourite dishes. Rose still favoured grandsons but knowing very well how dear Jessica was to her husband, she made an effort to indulge this granddaughter, too.

"Your job is to feed George four ounces of formula before bed and watch him sleep. He has to listen to 'Twinkle, Twinkle, Little Star' to fall asleep. If you can't sing, just play it on Spotify. He usually sleeps through the night but if he wakes up, rock him a bit and play the lullaby again. Check his nappies; if it's 'Number Two,' change him."

"If you only need me to watch George sleep, why do you ask me here so early? Can I go back and hang out with Grandpa?"

"NO! You need to watch how mum looks after George and learn. She's on day shift now, and you are going to take over in the evening."

"Why don't you ask Maryanne to help? I am sure she is more experienced with babies than I am." Jessica still could not believe Janice struggled to entrust her baby to the capable helpers.

"I would have if mum didn't enslave her around the house from early morning. I doubt she has any energy left after she's finished with cleaning the kitchen after dinner. You're an artist; you hardly sleep at night. Your responsibility is to watch George sleep - how hard can that be? Come on, sis, please help me. What do you think I would choose, between spending the night watching my baby, or watching my dead father-in-law in his coffin, if I have a choice?"

"It's called jet-lag. I do sleep at night, just not when I am here."

Despite her protest, Jessica did feel sorry for her sister. Besides taking care of baby George, Janice had to help to prepare Patrick Lee's funeral, as she was the wife of his eldest son. According to the indigenous traditions, the coffin in which the deceased reposed in had to be kept in the living room. The immediate female family of the deceased had to dress in a special linen costume, kneel and cry overnight, the louder, the better.

Jessica laughed for a moment imagining her sister fake crying her heart out for her late father-in-law. She had no doubt that Janice was going to put on a performance that would be worthy an Oscar. She recalled the countless times her cheeky sister had used the same trick to get both of them out of trouble with her parents throughout their childhood. Although, it would only be the beginning of the funeral, as the service was to last for three long days. It was an event for the whole village, as important as a wedding, if not more, depending on the hierarchy of the deceased. The preparations began eight to ten days before Patrick passed away after the doctor had confirmed that his time was about to come to its end. A temporary venue was to be built with bamboo scaffolding near the entrance of the village, where the coffin in which Patrick was lying would be displayed for at least two nights for the villagers to come to pay their respect. During that time, there would be a religious ceremony to give blessings to both the deceased as well as to his surviving families members.

Jessica drew her drifted thoughts back to reality. She had to plan her week ahead efficiently after fulfilling her family obligation to attend Patrick Lee's funeral. The main purpose of her trip was to meet up with the Chinese Medicine Department of a local university. Her sponsor in London had initiated a collaboration with the Chinese University of Hong Kong to create an art project on portraying trees and plants in Hong Kong and Southern China that had medicinal value and use. There was no coincidence here as the organisation wanted to fully optimise Jessica's connections and knowledge in the Far East to conduct more interesting and unprecedented researches. The Botanical Society also wanted to expose their name and works to the Chinese community to attract more foreign funding as China gradually became an economic superpower.

The staff and senior students would make an introduction of certain common plants and trees used in Chinese medicine to Jessica. In return, Jessica would act as a guide to whereabouts they could find them, especially near Ma's village. It was going to be a year-long project as Jessica would have to return a few times to record, in drawing, the growth of the species in their own habitats. The works could at times be tedious, lonely and annoying, given the nearly unbearable humidity during the hot and rainy seasons.

George made a cry and Jessica jerked up. She breathed a sigh of relief after George soothed himself back to sleep, sucking his own thumb. Looking at the innocent baby who was likely having a sweet dream, Jessica doubted the little boy had any idea of how lucky he was by winning the 50/50 lottery and being born as a boy in an indigenous family. She still remembered the series of village activities to celebrate George's arrival. A lantern lighting ceremony was held, where firecrackers were fired, and a lion dance was performed. A lavish banquet was laid out for the whole village to enjoy local delicacies such as suckling pigs, abalones, shark fins, etc. As the property price in Hong Kong had surged through the roof in recent decades, so had the value of a baby boy as he would be entitled to the right of 'Ding,' meaning the right of a male descendant, which would allow him to build a three-story house on a piece of land that was free of charge. The difference between a boy and a girl was millions of dollars, literally.

CHAPTER THREE

Jessica and her family were greeted by a sea of white when her father's seven-seater van arrived at the Shing Lei village, where Lee's clan was based. For most cultures, white, which was a symbol of purity and lifelong loyalty, was the colour of a wedding. While here, white was the colour of the funeral, the colour of death. In recent years Jessica found herself experiencing some reverse cultural shock, whenever she returned from the U.K. for some family occasions. She had to remind herself that this was her roots, that's how things were done where she's from.

Jaguar manoeuvred the van through the crowds and parked at a spot and at an angle which would allow the vehicle to get out smoothly when it was time to leave. It took years to master such skills as there were few official car parks in the countryside where every village household owned more than one car.

As soon as Jessica stepped out of the van, she was assaulted by waves of screams and howls of mourners. The sounds of suona and drums playing at the funeral ritual became deafening when they approached the village hall. Stepping into the funeral service, Jessica tried to search for Janice and see how she was faring from the whole ordeal. She had to cover her mouth to stop herself from laughing when she saw Barbara Lee, Patrick's wife, beating her chest and pulling her hair while screaming for her late husband to 'take her with him,' complaining he was so cruel to leave her behind. Yet, just ten steps away from the dramatic display of her affection for her late husband, Patrick's mistresses and bastard children were also dressed in mourning clothes to bid their final farewell to the once most powerful figure in the Lee family.

Patrick Lee was infamous for keeping a handful of mistresses. Because of his family wealth and him being the eldest son of the eldest son back for many generations, he was the King in the family. He could afford to feed and house for all his children and wives. Since the High Court had ruled that bastard sons of an indigenous of a male descendant would also be entitled to a 'Ding,' those who had been fathered by Patrick gradually took root in the village.

Barbara was a crafty woman and cunning at power play with her husband's mistresses. In order to keep the peace in the marriage, Patrick allowed Barbara an extravagant lifestyle and instructed his mistresses to keep a convivial distance from her. Now, with the passing of the giant, everyone looked forward to seeing how the power would be reshuffled.

There were rumours going around that Patrick's mistresses had already hired an army of inheritance lawyers to fight for what they thought was rightfully theirs. Despite owning a vast fortune, it was not a common practice for the indigenous culture to leave a will which was considered as bad luck and even a curse to the living. Therefore, there were often years of battle in courts among the offspring and lovers of the dead.

It had been a while since Jessica attended a local funeral, especially one as grand as Patrick Lee's. The last one she'd been to was for the grandfather of her best friend, Ailsa, in London. Compared to a village funeral, the service in Europe was much cosier. The ceremony was a solemn one where silent tears were shed, memories of the deceased were shared in humorous and touching speeches. Meanwhile, back in the villages, even at death, it was an occasion to show off one's status and power. Sometimes, a funeral would be even more elaborate than a wedding, if the deceased was someone powerful like Patrick.

One of the very important reasons for the preference to have a male heir was that after the funeral, the strong men in the family would help to carry the coffin, up on the hill to where a gravestone would be built. The older generation was keen on having a male descendant to walk them on their last journey on earth. The stone would usually be erected at a prime spot and look over the ocean. It was believed that the ancestors of the indigenous clan would be looking over the shoulders of the living down in the village from above.

The immediate family members of Patrick were all covered in hard, coarse, and skin-irritating linen on top of their mourning white clothes to express their respect for him. Jessica knew that her sister had sensitive skin, she could imagine how uncomfortable it must be for her. Even though Janice did not have to carry the coffin up onto the hill, she was still expected to kneel and kowtow on the ground every ten steps she took from the service towards the bottom of the hill. It was going to be a very, very long day for her.

"Holy Moly! Uncle Jimmy is here, talking to Patrick's mistresses. He must be trying to buy them out of their homes now that their man is gone," Jay whispered to Jessica and directed her attention to the small crowd gathering after the young and strong in the village commenced the transport of Patrick's coffin up to the hill where he was to rest ever after.

Jimmy was the second son of Jackson and the fraternal twin of Jessica's father, Jaguar. Jimmy always resented his two minutes late in arrival compared to his older brother, Jaguar, which cost him the throne in the Ma's kingdom to inherit the family fortune accumulated from generation after generation. Nevertheless, Jimmy refused to submit to fate. He was ambitious and determined to build his own empire. For years, when the 'Ding' right was still commonly traded, he bought them off one by one at a price which was considered dirt cheap at today's money, but an enormous sum to a teenager who was about to enter adulthood. Jimmy then auctioned the accumulative pieces of land to the highest bidder among the land developers. With the fortune from land banking, Jimmy started his own company to lead projects developing the countryside of the city. He was acquainted with many government officials and played golf with major players in real estate. Jimmy could not miss the opportunity to get his hands on to the mouth-watering Lee properties, which spread across some of the most sought-after lands in the area. He was positive that most of Lee's mistresses and bastard sons would be willing to cash off and move away from Queen B - Barbara.

Still thinking of Janice, Jessica murmured some response to Jay as she had no interest in any family saga, whether it's in her own village or someone else's.

"Sis, I would like you to meet someone while you are still in town. Hmm, actually I would like to you be around when I make the announcement. I am still not sure if I should, but I think I owe it to Tony and mum before we get married."

Jessica realised Jay's gossips were only the opening to something much more personal and serious.

"Getting married?" Jessica's mouth dropped. Once she resumed her composure, she had to admire her baby brother's courage. "Oh, Jay, I wish you the best of luck of bringing the topic up to mum and dad... and yes, count me in for a seat on the groom's side of guests."

"Both Tony and I are going to be grooms. No bride in a gay marriage, capiche?"

"Excuse my ignorance." Jessica gestured a kowtow to Jay to ask for his forgiveness.

The LGB trend was still in its budding phase in the U.K. as the English were still quite conservative about one's sexual orientation. She had to remind herself to keep an open mind when it came to her brother's love life.

"Tony is the third generation from California. We can get married legally there. All his family will come to our wedding. I... am hoping you and Uncle Jakey will come." Jaguar's youngest brother, Jake, was considered the most liberal person in the family. He was even described as a hippy, given his occupation as a yoga teacher, and his favourite past time was meditation.

***

The next day Jay made a proper introduction of his fiancé, Tony, to Jessica. They met in a café near the university where Jessica had her collaboration with. She had to wrap up her visit with its Chinese Medicine Department and make a plan for her next, so she could report to her supervisor when she went back to London. Jessica cursed that there were often family matters that drew much of her attention away from her obligations with work. Yet, she didn't have much choice as Jay considered Jessica the representative of his family, given that she was the only one who truly loved him for who he was - and probably the only one who would behave courteously toward his partner-to-be.

Tony was strikingly handsome, well-mannered, and funny. Jessica could see why Jay fell for him. Damn, she could fall in love with Tony, too, if he'd liked women. Jessica sighed that most attractive men in town were gay. In any case, she was happy for her baby brother.

***

The following evening, the family had a meal together before Jessica took the late-night flight bound for Heathrow. Jessica had to see it as her parents' display of love for her; otherwise, there was little to convince herself for such sentiment.

"Mum, Dad…" Everyone paused eating when Jay opened his mouth. It was rare that he had anything to say at dinner. "Iiiiii… aaaaam getting… maaaaaarriiiiied, next month, in Caaaaaalifornia." Jay tended to stutter when he felt nervous.

Silence fell upon the dining table for a full minute…

"Oh, thank heaven and earth for having Jay turn around! Joanne, let's go to the village temple together first thing in the morning to burn a few more incense to thanks our ancestors." Jessica's mum, Helen, stood up and made a quick prayer upwards, overwhelmed with joy that Jay had decided to bring a bride home. "Don't be silly about having a wedding in California. Your father is the village chief; we are obliged to hold a big banquet and invite EVERYBODY. If the girl's family insists on having the wedding in the U.S., we can have both, we are easy. Real easy!" Helen started to do a mental headcount and the number of tables that would be required to seat everyone.

"No, Mum, it's Tooooony I am going to marry. I told you guys a while ago about him. And that I knew from a young age that I do nooooooot like gggggggirls…"

"We are going to get married, legally, in the U.S. I am not expecting you guys to come to the wedding, I am just letting you know…" Jay calmed down after getting the most important words out.

An even longer minute of silence fell upon the dining table before a fist hit the table that made Jessica jumped.

"Don't you ever dare to bring your 'wife' back here in THIS village. You don't care about face, but I DO!" Jaguar, red-faced and boiling hot, pointed his finger at his youngest son while making his position very clear. He stood up and stormed out of the dining room. Dinner was over for everyone.

"I am not asking you to welcome Tony into the family. I am just asking you to let us have ours." Jay's voice was turning to a whisper as his courage diminished along with the sentence. Helen looked at him with many disappointments shown on her face. She shook her head and left the room, too, to go after the dragon to calm him down.

"Can you talk to them for me, please? They love you the most," Jay pleaded with Joe.

"Don't touch me, you faggot! It's your own shit, clean it up yourself." Joe swiped his brother's arm off his shoulders like he was some annoying flies. He picked up his bottle of beer and walked out to the living room. He put his feet up and turned the TV on as if nothing had happened.

Watching the scene unfolding in front of her, Jessica didn't know what's worse - to be born a girl in an indigenous family or a boy who didn't like girls.

Chapter Four

Jaguar's cigarette was puffing while his chest rose up and down rapidly. He quickly retreated from the dining room before he did something he might regret later. In recent years, he often made a detour to the master bedroom to calm himself down, giving an exit to the troubled child to escape from his rage through the house to the garden. From the balcony, he could spy on anyone coming and going, in and out of the house, knowing when he could get out of the jail of his own fury. Indeed, he was beyond furious. It was one thing that Jay admitted that he did not like girls, but getting married to a man? He must be out of his mind and probably caught up by the current trend in various countries where same-sex marriage was gradually being legalised. But Jay should know very well that the village had its own law. How could he ever face anyone if his own son married a faggot? Jaguar hit his fist hard on the concrete of the balcony fence when the picture of the ridicule appeared on his mind. He ignored the agony and the blood oozing out of the capillaries on his right hand. He needed the pain to numb his anger.

"Please don't get upset. I think he's just trying his luck. He's not really going to marry that man if we say NO…" Helen walked into their bedroom moments after Jaguar did and tried to calm the dragon.

Jay was her youngest son as well as her favourite. Jay had always been a sweet boy since he was young, although she had never suspected that the soft, feminine side of him was, in fact, a telling sign of his sexual orientation. And she knew very well deep down her husband loved every single one of their children. He had to maintain a façade of a strong leader who respected traditions and safeguard his reputation for who he was in the village. He was the eldest son of the leading family in the Ma's clan. Lots of people looked up to him and relied on his leadership on important matters.

"That's your fault! You have always been too soft on him. You should have been stricter with him and raise him up to the man he is supposed to be." Jaguar could not help but blame the first person who dared to come to talk to him. And of course, when it comes to the responsibility of nurturing children, it lied one hundred per cent on the mother's side. A father's role was to provide, to bring food to the table, and place a sturdy roof over everyone's head; a role that Jaguar took very seriously and believed he had tried his best in fulfilling.

Jaguar knew very well from a young age that he had won the lottery by coming to the world two minutes earlier than his fraternal twin brother, Jimmy. The prize included but was not limited to, acres of lands, dozens of detached houses, millions in cash and kilos of gold as well as jewels passing down the lineage for generations. Yet, he understood the power brought by the vast fortune and the status of being the head of the leading family, came with responsibility.

He ignored the advice from his father Jackson to study aboard, which Jimmy gladly followed, and instead, he learned by choice, the trade of construction ever since he reached the legal age to pick up a shovel. To him, that's honest work. The bowl of rice he earned after hours of sweating from labour tasted sweeter. He spent years working alongside the villagers he hired today, in digging holes on the roads, wielding steel for new buildings, fixing roofs for the elderly… before he felt ready to start his own construction company. Jaguar had not only acquired the skills and knowledge of the trade, but he had also earned the respect from everyone in the village that he's a worthy village leader and not just one who only earned the title through his pedigree.

He employed most of the village. Because of his thorough knowledge of the trade, he often found the right job for the right calibre and personality. He paid everyone a fair wage and was generous with sharing the profit. Jaguar knew it's the best way to keep the village happy and united. The only regret was the little time he had left for his own children. He should have known better - that Helen was too soft of a mother to be relied on raising strong boys. Not every woman was a tiger mum like his. Being a grandma now, Rose was still nicknamed as 'the mum who has thorns;' even her own sons were fearful of her.

"I read in an article recently in the newspaper which suggested that sexual orientation was genetics. There's really nothing we have or have not done to change the fact that our son likes boys." Helen's voice drew Jaguar back to the dire situation at his doorsteps.

"Genetics?! Who in our family do you know is gay?" Jaguar raised both his voice and finger at Helen, who was used to sheltering her children from their father's temper while trying her best to smooth things out.

"Alright, alright, the faults are all mine. Just don't get yourself all worked up. Mind your heart." Helen gently reminded her husband of his condition with high blood pressure. Despite being in construction and as active as someone half his age, Jaguar's smoking habit did not help, especially in the last decade when he approached his sixties.

"Gay or not, he's our son, our youngest son. We need to be gentle when it comes to our children's love affairs. These young people are very delicate and easily blinded by love. Most of all, we don't want to repeat our mistake with Joanne… every time I see her staying home by herself on weekends, I blame us for being too harsh on her."

Jaguar immediately softened up when Helen mentioned Joanne with tears in her eyes.

Their second daughter, Joanne, was an introvert. She had always been self-sufficient. She learned to be independent at a young age when her mother was busy chasing after the little ones. She excelled academically at school and was brilliant with mathematics. She picked up accounting skills from textbooks she borrowed from the public library near the village and taught herself bookkeeping. She started working as a family accountant well before she earned her qualification as an accountant. She kept everything to herself and barely talked to anyone, both in the house or in the village. Therefore, when Joanne turned nineteen and came home one day telling her mother that she was pregnant, it came as a shock that neither Helen nor Jaguar would ever think of even in their wildest imagination. Their mature, intelligent and obliging second daughter had been fooling around with boys and got herself knocked up! Worse, Joanne never uttered a word about who the father might be. Outraged, Jaguar dragged her to a shady clinic to have an abortion, as Helen suspected that their daughter was nearly six months pregnant and the baby could not be removed at a hospital legally. Unfortunately, the butcher act by the barely legal doctor led to a significant blood loss for Joanne and permanent damage done to her womb that it was believed she could never get pregnant again for the rest of her life. Joanne had been physically weak ever since.

She became even quieter and kept her head down with studies then work. She never dated nor hung out with friends. She just stayed home and read. Helen deeply regretted what she and her husband had done to Joanne. They forced an abortion on her out of love, such that she could get married to a proper family and have legitimate children. They never expected the horrible, disastrous outcome, but it was entirely the fault of her, and her husband's doing.

There was a soft knocking on the door. Helen went and opened it and found her brother-in-law, Jake, standing in front of her. Jaguar saw the sight of his youngest brother, and his shoulders dropped.

"Let's talk in the study," he sighed and led Jake down the hallway.

"So, the boy is determined this time?" Jaguar knew Jay was serious when he sought help from his Uncle Jakey.

"Very," Jake replied.

Jake was adored by every single member of the family. He was the youngest son of Jackson and Rose. He always had that calm temperament in him that the older generation in the village insisted that Jake was some kind of Buddhist reincarnation. With that mystic persona about Jake, Rose, inclined to believe her son was some sort of saint, let him be and never pushed him to work and perform as she did with Jaguar and Jimmy. True to his nature, Jake was gentle with everyone. He loved reading philosophy and practised yoga and meditation from adolescence, without being influenced by any adult in his life. He had a partner who was also a yoga instructor but decided they would not have any children. No one ever imposed any family obligations on Jake. Instead, everyone went to him to seek wisdom or when they wanted to talk about things as if he was a shrink.

"I blame myself for not having spent enough time with him and teach him how to be a man," Jaguar sighed again. He sighed a lot when he was with his baby brother. Despite being the eldest, he sought comfort from Jake and consulted with him whenever he felt indecisive about something. His sighing was a sign of surrendering himself and dropping his guard, the strong façade he felt he had to put on around everyone else. With Jake, he knew he could show signs of weakness and his brother would never think any less of him.

"On the contrary, Jay is a very solid and wise kid. He is much stronger than most of the 'men' you know. He's been very clear with what he wants from Day One. You are shocked now because you have been in denial. You just need to open your heart, then you will see."

"How can I face the villagers if they find out my son is married to another man?" Jaguar suddenly felt as helpless as he was fearful of what everyone in the village would make of him if they knew he was the father of a homosexual.

"If you care less about what others in the village think, and more about how your son feels, believe me, you will live a much happier life." Jake rose and was ready to leave.

"Wait! Jake, don't go just yet. Do… you think you can try to talk some sense into Jay?" Jaguar begged his baby brother to help him out of the unimaginably embarrassing situation.

"I thought I have just talked some sense into you. I will be at my nephew's wedding. If you are not man enough to walk your son down the aisle, I will." Jake then opened the door of the study and found his niece, Jessica, with her hand in the air, about to knock the door.

"Hi, Uncle Jakey, I've come to say goodbye to Dad. I'm leaving for the airport."

Jake then pulled Jessica in for a hug and wished her a safe flight. "We will hang out more when you are back next time. A shame that I was away on a yoga retreat nearly the whole time you were here."

"It's alright. You didn't get the memo from Patrick that he was on his way out."

Jake gave a hearty laugh - he loved the sense of humour of his youngest niece.

Jaguar cleared his throat behind him. Jessica immediately stood taller and pulled a serious face. She said goodbye to her father and asked him to take care of himself and Helen.

"Who's going to drop you off at the airport? When will you come home next?" Although Jaguar did not spend much time with his children, there's nothing he loved more than having his whole clan at home.

"Jacqueline and Brother-in-law. Probably after summer. It will be the prime season for us to work in the U.K. when everything is blooming." Jessica was grateful for being able to spend the summer in Europe where the weather was beautiful, the days were long, and people were happy. After living abroad for a few years, she couldn't stand the heat and humidity back in the village anymore. Focusing on her work in England was the perfect summer escape for her.

CHAPTER FIVE

"How did you come back with a weekend duffel bag and end up leaving with two big suitcases? Are you sure they don't exceed the baggage limit?" Simon, Jessica's brother-law, was attempting to shut the trunk door several times without success. In the end, he had to move the shopping trolley and the cool box to the back passenger seat to make some room to fit Jessica's heavy bags.

"You can talk to your mother-in-law and ask her not to use me as everyone's courier to carry things to London." Jessica was certain Helen announced her visit to the whole village whenever she came home. Before the end of her stay, she would find two oversized suitcases sitting in her room with a detailed list of things to pass on to her cousins or neighbours who resided or studied near London. The 'things' ranged from light items such as cardigans, medicines that would otherwise require doctor prescriptions, to seriously heavy gadgets like laptops, rice cookers, etc. She deliberately did not bring back any suitcase, but each time her mother beat her by buying two brand new trunks. Jessica sold all of them at some marketplace in London. She saw the little income as her fee to haul everything across continents to reach her distant relatives. She also made it clear to the recipients if they did not collect by a deadline she would dispose of the parcels as she wished.

Jacqueline, Jessica's eldest sister, was sitting in the passenger seat next to her husband, while Jessica and Jay sat in the back. Now the initial terror of announcing the wedding news to his parents was over, Jay, now relaxed in his brother-in-law's car, excitedly talked about his wedding plans with the more open-minded members of his family.

"Tony's mum managed to secure an outdoor venue at the end of August. The weather will be perfect, and most of my friends in the fashion industry welcome the last break of their summer holiday before the beginning of the autumn-winter season. Uncle Jakey is going to walk me down the aisle. It's going to be awesome. These years he's been more of a father figure to me that Dad is. I am so happy that he said 'yes!'"

"Poor Jay, our parents won't be around at your wedding. I wish Dad fretted less over traditions. Everything is about 'face' to him. But don't worry, you will have your families there on your big day. Count all three of us in. I am sure Grandpapa would love to attend. Go talk to him tomorrow. I can't speak for Joanne, but I will try to convince Janice to go; it's a pity baby George is still too young to be the ring-bearer." Jessica tried to cheer her baby brother up.

"Speaking of traditions, I don't think Janice can go anywhere within the one hundred days after her father-in-law's funeral." Jay reminded his sister that she was being too optimistic to count on Janice's presence at his wedding.

"Well, you still have half a dozen of us witnessing your union with Tony. And mark my word, I suspect mum will soften up by then and show up in California at the last minute." Jessica had no doubt about their mother's presence at her favourite's child's wedding.

"I am sure Dad will change his mind if you can find Tony a trade that can benefit the whole village," Jacqueline joked. She believed if it wasn't the fact that Simon was a doctor, there was no way her father would let her marry a foreigner. She met her husband Simon, an Australian national, by accident or by fate when Simon had a quarrel with one of the villagers and went to seek help from the 'attorney' in the village.

Growing up on a farm in New South Wales, Simon could not stand the skyscrapers and density in the city. He chose to live in a village house in the countryside and commute between home and the hospital where he worked as a heart surgeon. Simon planned to stay in Hong Kong for only two years to complete his fellowship; he did not expect to meet the love of his life and had since lived in the Ma's village for over a decade. In the beginning, he rented a house from one of the villagers. He soon started to have quarrels with his landlord over who was responsible for certain house maintenance. To be fair to Simon, the house was falling apart. The real estate agent told Simon that the landlord would be responsible for the maintenance if needed. Simon loved the panoramic view he could enjoy from both the top floor balcony and the rooftop. He naively trusted what the agent promised him that the landlord would bear the cost of the handy jobs. After moving in, there had been no response from the landlord even over some urgently required repairs such as some chipping walls and leaking air conditioners. Simon had been footing the bills, then deducted from the rent. Soon the maintenance expenses exceeded that of the rent, and still, his landlord did not show any interest in helping. Simon asked around and learned Jacqueline's name from other expatriates living in the area. He went to her office one day and tried to seek the lawyer's help over his conflict with his landlord.

Despite being a daughter, Jacqueline knew her importance in the family. As a lawyer she not only helped her immediate family in everyday legal matters, and property transactions, all villagers came to her for help even with trivial matters whenever they couldn't understand certain clauses on some commercial documents. Jacqueline charged a very reasonable price, compared to what she could have made at a fancy law firm. She requested to use one of the one-story village houses close to the village office as her office to meet villagers or other clients if there were any. To show their appreciation, several of her uncles turned the old, tired village property into a professional-looking office for Jacqueline. She hired a couple of her cousins as her legal secretary and office manager.

The day when Simon came to find Jacqueline, both her assistants were out for lunch. Usually, Jacqueline would not receive anyone who had not made an appointment in advance, but her heart softened once she saw Simon's pleading face. Simon spilt out his frustrations while Jacqueline only listened to him half-heartedly. She was too distracted by Simon's shabby handsome face and his surfer physique. Whenever Simon had time off from the hospital, he would be surfing along the coast. His skin was tanned, and his hair turned ash-blond from exposure to the sun. He was tall, and his shoulders were broad while his waist was narrow. Jaqueline was daydreaming and picturing Simon carrying a surfboard on the beach when Simon drew her back to reality.

"Do you think I have any chance to negotiate with my landlord or should I start looking for another place to move to?" Simon loved his house despite the condition it was in, but he would choose to retreat as a last resort. Other foreigners advised him not to make an enemy out of an indigenous villager.

"Move? Of course not! Don't worry, I will be your representative and deal with your landlord." The last thing Jacqueline wanted was to have Simon moved away from the village.

Simon's landlord was her Uncle Brian, who was known for being tight with money. Brian let out a few of his houses to expatriates as they were willing to pay a premium for space and the view his houses offered. If he could get out of it, he would do the absolute minimum for his tenants. Jacqueline knew it was not the first time nor the last time Uncle Brian got complaints from the people who paid for his bills. She made the decision to help Simon, even if Uncle Brian was not willing to chip in. She could call on several other villagers who were her father's employees and owed her favours. So long as Simon stuck around for her to get to know him.

Simon thought it was a miracle that within two weeks, all the repairs in the house were done. The property was finally in good shape, and he loved it even more. He thought highly of the young lady who managed to get his landlord to give in. Indeed, he found her stunningly beautiful. Her big, brown eyes sparkled when she talked. She was strong in her head but soft in her features. She commanded with grace; exactly the type of woman he was attracted to. He went back to Jacqueline's office a few times, sometimes with a bouquet of flowers, to thanks her for saving him the confrontation with his landlord while getting the house back in good form. Jacqueline realised the doctor was too shy for his own good. In the end, she took the initiative to ask him out.

"So, now there's nothing left to fix in your house, do you have time to go out for dinner sometime?" Jacqueline saw Dr Simon break into a big smile. She knew that something amazing was going to happen.

Three years after Simon had knocked on Jacqueline's office for her assistance, they decided to tie the knot. The only challenge was there had never been a non-Chinese marriage in Ma's village. As the leading family, Jacqueline's father, Jaguar, was more traditional than any other father in the village. Jaguar at first did not take Simon seriously as he believed he was going back to Australia after he got bored of Hong Kong. He did not expect he was going to ask him for his daughter's hand. Jaguar tried to put forward different arguments to Jacqueline to convince her not to marry Simon.

However, Jaguar forgot his daughter was a lawyer. Jacqueline subtlety threatened her father that she would move to Australia with Simon if Jaguar did not give them his blessings. On the other hand, if Jaguar welcomed her fiancé into the family, she promised to stay in the village and continued to serve as the family attorney.

By then, Simon was not only in love with Jacqueline but also the city he's called home in the past four years. Simon was very happy to stay on when Jacqueline told him about her negotiation with Jaguar. It did not take much more convincing as Simon had also become the family physician, especially with Jaguar's heart condition that had developed in recent years. Half a decade on, everyone in the village loved having the couple around - one to consult for legal issues and the other for medical matters.

After seeing Jessica off at the security checkpoint, Jay asked Jacqueline and Simon if they could drop him off to the nearest train station. He would travel back to the city. He spent more time these days at Tony's apartment than back in the family house in the village. Joe had been getting ruder to him these days. He did not want to talk to or sometimes even being the same room as his baby brother.

His comments such as, 'Don't pass your AIDs to me!' or 'Have you been screwed in the ass yet this week?' deeply hurt Jay. Jay's gentle temperament and manners did not serve him well when he had to confront the arrogance and pomposity of his ignorant brother. Jaqueline felt sorry for Jay and was glad that Jay had found his true love. He was going to get married and moved away from the family; an institution that they grew up in but grew more apart from its traditional values.

As Simon pulled the car close to the subway station, suddenly all of their smartphones rang simultaneously. The trio looked at each other and quickly retrieved their respective phones. Their mother called Jay, and father did Jacqueline, while Simon's call was from grandpa Jackson. They answered their phones right away. They murmured a similar response to the mouthpiece and hung up.

"It's Grandma Rose..." they announced the same thing to each other at the same time.

Chapter Six

Simon sped at the absolute limit and drove everyone back to the village.

"Are they home or at the grandparents' house?" Jay was suddenly not sure where the accident occurred that resulted in Grandma Rose's slipping.

"The grandparents' house. Grandpa called Dad then rang Simon. That's how everyone operates. Inform the chief first before asking for professional help." Jacqueline reminded Jay that even someone as open-minded as their grandfather also chose to follow the village way.

Simon pulled the car up right outside the house of Rose and Jackson. Helen ran out of the house upon hearing the car engine and waved her children into the house. The trio rushed in, expecting to see Grandma Rose lying on the floor crying for help and cursing the parents for not calling for an ambulance. However, when they stepped into the living room, they found Grandma Rose sitting on the sofa drinking a cup of tea and chatting with her son.

"Mum, we thought it's some emergency. We nearly hit another car, trying to come back as soon as possible." Jacqueline was annoyed by how urgent her parents sounded on the phone and recalled the few close calls on the road just now.

"I told your mum and dad that they did not need to call an ambulance. I just sprained my ankle, that's all. My hip is not broken." Grandma Rose took another sip of her tea, but her face grimaced when she tried to lift her leg.

"Sorry for rushing you back like this. I hate getting in the middle between your grandma and your dad. That's why I called Simon so he can take a look first then we can decide if we should take Rose to the hospital." Jackson felt guilty about causing a scene, but he knew he would feel better if Rose could get some medical attention. Rose had slipped when she was mopping the floor. Their helper was on holiday and had gone back to the Philippines for a week. Rose couldn't stand the dust after two days and insisted on mopping the floor herself, but she didn't really have the strength to dry the mop properly anymore. The tiles also took a long time to dry in the high humidity of the hot season. Rose did not pay attention and slid across the floor for a distance. Luckily, she'd grabbed onto the arm of the sofa and avoided landing on her hip or worse, her head. The sofa took much of her weight, but she'd still hurt her ankle as a result.

"Well, it's fortunate that it's not an emergency. Let me take a look at Rose's ankle." Simon had the authority of a doctor, and everyone kept quiet while he inspected Rose's leg. He asked a few questions and checked a few spots to make sure there were no other injuries. A few minutes later, Simon confirmed that Rose could wait until the next morning to visit the clinic. Meanwhile, he would help her put on some bandage to stabilise the ankle and lighten the swelling.

"It shouldn't be anything serious, but it may take a while and effort to get back to how it was before. I am sure your GP would suggest you have physiotherapy and maybe have some dietary change to increase your calcium intake. Or taking a supplement to strengthen your bones. You will have to listen and follow what the doctor says."

It was delightful for everyone to watch how Grandma Rose, usually a fierce figure, nodded her head like a student at every sentence, Dr Simon said to her.

And the term 'physiotherapy' caught Jay's attention. He volunteered to take Grandma Rose to the clinic the next day. "A friend of mine is an experienced physiotherapist. I will take grandma to the doctor and talk to him."

Both Helen and Jaguar were pleasantly surprised and touched by Jay's gesture. They both believed Jay must have come to his senses and tried to make it up to his family.

***

The elevator door opened on the top floor and Jacqueline was greeted enthusiastically by the receptionist. Most staff knew who Jacqueline was. She was not a full-time employee, but she had her own office. She was also the niece of their boss.

"Hi, Jacqueline. They are ready in the conference room for you. Would you like the usual? An Americano and a glass of water on the side?" Evelyne, Jimmy's personal assistant, handed some folders over to Jacqueline and invited Jacqueline to join her down the hallway while giving a signal to Irene the receptionist to prepare Jacqueline's beverages.

Jacqueline loved being in her uncle Jimmy's office. It was such a contrast from the village. The atmosphere vibrated with energy and excitement. Everyone walked with a purpose here. It was the only place where she could wear her tailor-made power suits. Her appearance fitted in perfectly into the environment and the sea view office her uncle very kindly reserved for her exclusive use whenever she visited. And she did visit quite often, especially in the past year when Uncle Jimmy was negotiating important deals with the big real estate developers.

Jacqueline respected and admired her Uncle Jimmy. Being the second son in the Ma's, Jimmy was not the first in line to inherit the family's fortune. He invested the little he was given by his father and late grandfather and built an enterprise of his own. Yet, the best thing about Uncle Jimmy, in Jacqueline's opinion, was that he did not favour his son over his two daughters because of their gender difference. Her cousin, Anthony, was the eldest, but his two younger sisters, Susan and Sarah, were more intelligent and ambitious. Anthony was talented in art, like his grandfather and cousin Jessica but had no interest in management. His father encouraged him to take on interior design and architecture. Anthony thrived in both and was the head designer as well as the architect for his father's property developing business. Susan and Sarah were the company's COO and CFO, respectively. Uncle Jimmy made it very clear that he would pick his successor by merit. The most capable of his staff in his company would take over as the CEO the day he retired.

Uncle Jimmy was always fond of his eldest niece and talked Jacqueline into joining his company and work as their in-house lawyer. His business was to urbanise the countryside. He foresaw the city would soon run out of space to build housing to house the growing population. He had been acquiring the Ding rights from villagers who could not afford to build a house and would rather cash out from the privilege they were born with.

Despite Jacqueline very much loving and wanting to join her uncle and have a proper career of her own, she was unconditionally loyal to her own father. In the end, they compromised that Jacqueline would work as a legal consultant for Uncle Jimmy. He hired a junior lawyer to do the footwork and follow Jacqueline's instructions when she was out of the office. Jaguar agreed with the arrangement as he believed Jacqueline would help the villagers to get a fair price from his brother. He loved his brother, was empathetic about his position but also understood that Jimmy was determined while also being power and wealth-hungry. He relied on Jacqueline to keep an eye on his baby brother to make sure he would not sell out his own clan.

"Hey Jacqueline, we are just about to start, take a seat." Uncle Jimmy was always happy to see her.

Jacqueline also got along well with her two cousins. She admired them and at the same time envied them for having Uncle Jimmy as their father, who did not favour their brother over them. Susan then took over and updated everyone on her initial negotiations with each of the major real estate developers in the city. Jacqueline had drawn up a draft letter of intention and asked Susan to present each of the firms with a list of conditions. Each of them was to sign it before they proceed to the next phase.

Uncle Jimmy bought up a number of small properties from Patrick Lee's mistresses and bastard sons. Patrick Lee tried to keep his concubines away from his wife Barbara, so all the lands were strategically located at a distance from the main village. The lands came to a decent commercial size and had pleasant surroundings. Patrick Lee's mistresses and children had no desire to stick around after he was gone, so Uncle Jimmy paid each of them a fair price, and Sarah the CFO, had done the analyses. She forecasted the investment would bring them a very lucrative return. Susan was in charge of talking to each of the developers who were interested in building villas in an exclusive location adjacent to both hills and water. It was just one of the many similar projects that Uncle Jimmy had in recent years. In no time, he had built himself an empire, and his speciality was to flip rural land into money printing luxury properties.

***

"Grandma, this is my friend Chi Kin. He is a very experienced physiotherapist and works at the hospital on the Peak. I have asked him to do me a favour and come to help you with your treatment. Now come, you have promised the doctor and Simon that you would follow his instructions and do the work to speed up your recovery."

Jay brought his friend Chi Kin to his grandparents' house the following day after Grandma Rose's visit to the clinic. Rose's doctor had made a similar diagnosis as Simon did and true to his predictions, the doctor had prescribed mostly physiotherapies to help Rose to get back on her feet. The doctor wrote a reference letter and asked Jay if they needed some recommendations. Jay explained to the doctor about the arrangement with his friend, and their family doctor was satisfied and saw them out of his office.

"Hello, Mrs Ma, my name is Chi Kin. I am going to take good care of you, and you will be running and dancing again in no time. Jay told me what a great dancer you are, and I can't wait to see how you swirl and spin in no time."

Rose found herself blushing. She could not believe how handsome and charming the physiotherapist her youngest grandson brought home was. She did love dancing and could master all the ballroom dances. In their retirement years, she often went to social dance occasions with Jackson. Jackson adored all forms of art and fell in love with Rose the first time he saw her move. She was elegant and full of confidence. Jackson was a bit intimidated by Rose's strong character. Yet, he was an overseas educated gentleman, and all ladies were charmed by his manners. He was thrilled to hear a 'yes' from Rose when he finally mustered the courage to ask her out. The rest was then history.

"I will teach you so you can go charm some ladies if you can get me back on my feet in less than a month. Tell me, young man, have you got someone in your life yet? If not, one of my granddaughters is single. She is a bit shy but still good looking. She will make a good wife."

Jay immediately knew Grandma Rose was talking about Joanne, the family spinster. He laughed and stole a quick look at Chi Kin, who casually dismissed Grandma Rose with ease. "Oh, thanks for offering to introduce me to your granddaughter, how kind. But, no thank you, I have already found the love of my life."

"Well, you must bring your lucky lady and come to meet me one day. My eyes are the sharpest in the village. I can tell you right away whether she will make a good wife for you." Rose was eager to give her motherly help to the young gentleman she just met.

"We'll see, but first let's work on your leg and ankle. I will show you some exercises, and you follow. Before the end of the session, I will massage your ankle with some medical cream to speed up the recovery." Chi Kin spoke to Rose very gently, and Rose turned to that little girl again and nodded away to Chi Kin's instructions.

"If I do well, you will give me extra time on the massage part, deal?" Rose's eyes sparkled when she pictured Chi Kin's graceful hands working on her feet.

"You've got a deal, young lady," Chi Kin cheered Grandma Rose on.

Jay, standing in a corner, took in the scene in front of him and broke into a big smile. He silently thanked the universe for making his grandma slip.

CHAPTER SEVEN

"Pop, pop, pop, pop, pop." Uncle Jimmy, Susan, Sarah, Anthony, and Jacqueline each popped open a bottle of champagne to celebrate. They'd just sealed a deal with the biggest property developer in the city to collaborate on a project to develop the combined pieces of land Jimmy had recently acquired in Shing Lei Village, from Patrick Lee's mistresses and their bastard children. The development would allow the building of fifty luxurious villas, each with its own swimming pool and garage. The villas would be built on a gentle cliff looking out to the sea. It was isolated from the village which would set itself aside as a luxury landmark in the area, and a different level of living. Yet, the location was still close enough to a highway that connected its residents with the city in under an hour. The project was expected to bring the company the largest revenue and profit to date.

Moreover, the company had pieces of land on hand that would provide at least two other similar opportunities. Jimmy and his children were not only celebrating the deal they had just closed but had begun a new chapter that would take what they had built from scratch to the level of the major players in the city.

Jacqueline appreciated that she was included as part of the family to pop open one of the champagne bottles.

Looking at the crowd that squeezed into the conference room, Jacqueline was in awe at what Uncle Jimmy had achieved, with the help of mainly his daughters, her cousins. She remembered nearly a decade ago, Uncle Jimmy started his company from one of the container offices back in the village. She had just started practising law while both Susan and Sarah, who were only one year apart in age, returned from graduate schools one after the other. Uncle Jimmy had never doubted his daughters' ability solely because they were girls. Instead, he encouraged them to go out and negotiate with men as if they were equal.

No one in the village had anticipated such achievements from Jimmy, the second son from the leading Ma family. Attention and hope were the privileges for the eldest, the first in line to inherit everything from the lineage. Today the office was located on the top floor of a prestigious building in the city's financial district. Uncle Jimmy had over one hundred employees and would need to hire more staff for the coming projects.

Jacqueline, at times like this, found herself in this bittersweet moment, when on the one hand she was proud of her uncle but at the same time envious of her cousins to be born into such an open-minded home. She tried to draw herself back to the current moment and reminded herself it was a joyful occasion.

She only had a sip of her champagne, thinking of the baby growing in her tummy. She and Simon had tried for years to start a family but without much luck. In her late thirties, when she was about to give up on ever going to be a mother, she was over the moon when she found herself pregnant several months ago. She had just safely passed the first trimester, and all blood tests came back with normal results, and they were going to have a girl. The scene in front of her gave her hope that her baby girl would have a fair chance in this world, just like her aunts.

***

"You are doing great. That is… very well. You are doing great. Beautiful!" Chi Kin cheered Grandma Rose along when she walked from one end of the dining table to another. Chi Kin had this incredible charm over Grandma Rose that, at the end of the first week of the physiotherapy, she was able to put weight onto her feet. Now towards the end of the second week, she started to do light exercise of walking.

Chi Kin did some homework after consulting with Jackson about Rose's favourite pieces of dance music. He downloaded all of them and compiled them into a playlist that lasted for a bit over an hour - the duration of their session. The music took Rose down memory lane to when she was young and vibrant and made her want to dance. It seemed to do magic to trigger her body cells to work together. Rose was motivated by the rhythms and swung her body along with the beats. Soon she was itching to move her feet. Chi Kin encouraged her to follow his steps and repeat certain moves that had been modified from his recovery programmes.

Jay came with him every time and told Rose that he would keep her company and be her cheerleader. He was touched by Chi Kin's effort in making Grandma Rose exercise at ease and with so much joy.

"Oh, this is fun! And I am doing marvellously. Ain't I, Jay?" Grandma Rose was proud of her progress while having so much fun with Chi Kin. She had never imagined that doing exercise with a physiotherapist could be so enjoyable. The music that Chi Kin played for her and the way he talked to her made her feel ten years younger. She determined to frequent more social dance occasions once she fully recovered from her fall. And she adored this young man brought home by Jay. He was so gentle and kind to her. How thoughtful he was to play all her favourite music in order to get her ass up and start exercising? Oh, how she wished he was one of her grandchildren such that she could see him more often, instead of only one month until her sessions ended.

Although Jackson did not say anything, and he usually spent his time in the garden, he knew exactly what was going on. He caught many times how Jay and Chi Kin looked at each other. The way their fingers entwined and lingered a bit too long when they passed things to one another. Jackson had never been revolted by the idea that his youngest grandson was gay. He knew the world had changed a lot since he was a young man himself. He vowed to love him just as he was. He also came to like Tony, or Chi Kin, which he believed was his Chinese name, who was so sweet to Rose that the usual 'grandma with thorns' was totally smitten by him. He thought it was a smart move of Jay, to win the heart of the queen before working on the king, Jaguar. If there's one person in the world the village chief would listen to, it's his mother.

***

Jessica jerked awake from a deep sleep. She thought she had a nightmare until she registered her phone's ringtone. She glanced at the clock, it was 3 a.m. Her heart started pumping hard. Someone must have died at home.

None of her family would wake her up in the middle of the night for any emergency, knowing the time difference and that there was little she could do to help with her being on the other side of the world. Jessica took a closer look at the caller ID; it was Mabel. Mabel was her best childhood friend. Her family was not indigenous, but her father had been employed in the village to work as an engineer for her father. Jessica and Mabel were in the same class since Primary One and had been best girlfriends growing up. Mabel was married to one of the big families in the village and was already a mother of three.

As they grew older, Jessica found more and more difference between Mabel and herself. If it weren't for the fact they had been close since childhood, she would not have been friends with Mabel today. Mabel was everything she disagreed with the traditional value system in the village. Mabel had always been jealous about how 'affluent' the indigenous people were and decided her goal was to marry into one of the big families in the village - and Mabel did. She married one of Jessica's distant cousins at the age of twenty-three. Unfortunately, in Mabel's opinion, all her three children were girls. According to her, girls were of no use; they were worth nothing.

Nevertheless, she convinced herself that she was only in her late twenties, so she could keep going, and sooner or later, she would have a son, an heir. During Jessica's last visit, Mabel was thrilled to share with her the news that finally, she was pregnant with a boy. She was safely into her fourth month of pregnancy, and her in-laws were so excited that they had planned a series of festivities to celebrate as soon as their grandson was born. They also promised Mabel to gift her money and a house as her rewards. Hence, Jessica could not imagine what the call could be about except Mabel's pregnant brain had forgotten the time zones difference they were in. Jessica went on and tapped the red hang-up button.

Only within minutes, the phone rang again – it was still Mabel. Jessica finally answered reluctantly.

"Babe, you've forgotten I am already back in London. It's three in the morning. Call me back in eight hours." She was about to hang up but was greeted by Mabel's sobbing voice.

"It's gooooone. My… boy…. iiiiiiis… goooo… ne." Mabel was out of breath from crying, and Jessica could hardly make out the words she was saying. Yet, Jessica got the message; Mabel had lost her baby, her baby boy that she had waited and prayed for years to have.

"Oh, babe, I am so sorry, how did it happen? I thought everything had settled, and you are well into your second trimester?" Jessica had limited knowledge about pregnancy. She only knew that most of the time, a pregnancy was considered normal and safe once the expecting mother had passed her first trimester.

"I can't do it anymore. I can't do it…" Mabel continued to beg on the other end of the receiver.

"Ok, ok, you don't have to do anything you don't want to. Tell me what's going on." Jessica tried her best to calm Mabel down.

"I was hit by a stabbing pain in the middle of the night, then the bleeding… There was so much blood, Jessica, the blood was everywhere. Then my baby boy's gone…"

Jessica tried to block away from the horrible picture as Mabel described it. She was heartbroken to hear her friend cry like that and to learn about her miscarriage at five months pregnant.

"Kenneth wants me to do IVF again as soon as I recover from the miscarriage. I don't want to do it, I don't want to do it anymore. But he swears he's going to divorce me if I can't give him a boy in the next three years. I have already gone through two IVF's, had three miscarriages and three abortions because they were girls… Kenneth suggested we have it next in Thailand where we can screen for gender in advance. But I really can't stand it, all the injections and surgeries…"

"Oh my God, I had no idea you've gone through all that…" Jessica covered her mouth and could not believe what Mabel had just told her. It was even more disgusting that her cousin Kenneth threatened his wife with ending their marriage if she could not produce a male heir.

"I am sure he's just bluffing. He's not actually going to divorce you for that. You have three children together, and you are a great mum. He'd be a fool to do that. And Grandma Rose can always talk some senses into his big head." Jessica didn't know what to say; somehow she thought of her fearless grandma who could without a doubt, let Kenneth have a taste of his own medicine.

"Girls are worthless to these people. A boy is worth what, twenty, thirty million these days? And it will be even more by the time they grow up. Kenneth said he's willing to invest in the expensive fertility treatments to have as many boys as possible. I am not a pig, Jessica. I am not a pig…" Mabel lost her voice and started sobbing again.

Jessica's body trembled with anger. She took a long, deep breath and tried to focus on the task on hand. It would be hours before she could finally drop her head back onto her pillow. She was exhausted but unable to fall asleep. Her stomach sickened with the thoughts of the many operations that Mabel would have to go through in the years to come. Despite her protest, she had no doubt her childhood best friend would bend to her cousins' demand and go with whatever it took to give birth to a boy, and more. And Mabel's 'these people' had struck a chord in Jessica's heart. 'These people' were her clan, her families.

CHAPTER EIGHT

"Help me go check on her, please. She sounded really bad on the phone. I don't want her to think there's no way out. And you may want to talk some sense into Kenneth - he can't force his wife into a pregnancy if she does not want to." Jessica pleaded with Janice to go and talk to Mabel, worried that she might hurt herself.

"Didn't mum teach us not to interfere with another family's business, especially meddling between a husband and his wife?" Janice had her hands full, and the last thing she wanted was to get involved in another family saga. She had had enough recently from her own husband's side of the family. Her late father-in-law's mistresses and bastard children had sold their houses and lands to Uncle Jimmy at a premium to build some luxury villas. With the money, they moved out of the village and settled in the city happily. His living wife, Janice's mother-in-law, on the one hand, was jealous of her late husband's mistresses who had the freedom to come and go. On the other hand, she was now out of enemies to play politics with and gossip about on a daily basis. She did not really mourn for the death of her husband but was miserable when his mistresses were leaving the village, and her, one by one.

The mistresses and their children were still in the fight for more inheritance, but they did not need to interact with Barbara directly. They hired some fancy lawyers who were very experienced in disputes like theirs. The legal battles kept Barbara occupied and fed her with stories to tell to her fellow villagers. The rest of the time, Barbara directed most of her attention and bitterness to everyone at home. She constantly picked on Janice, on nearly everything; the way she raised baby George, the way she cooked, the way she managed the household. Everything Janice did was not good enough, and nothing she did was enough. The worst accusation was that Janice was still unable to become pregnant with another boy now that George was nearly one. She also doubted if her daughter-in-law had been treating her son right.

The fact was, Janice was pregnant lately. When she found out it was a girl from a blood test at eleven weeks, she decided to terminate the pregnancy, in secret. Her husband was no Uncle Jimmy, so she believed she was doing 'this girl' favour by not bringing her into the world. She could do much better in the next life with a different family. Besides, she did not want to weaken her position and agenda to become a powerful mum with a handful of male heirs in the leading Lee family. She was still in her early thirties and had years ahead before she'd become too old to bear children anymore. She knew she could try again in two to three months. And if she had a girl again, she would consider going to a fertility treatment overseas where it allowed her to screen the gender in advance. In other words, she had a similar attitude and idea as Kenneth. She thought Mabel should just toughen up. *If you cannot beat the game, join it, play it, and exploit it.*

"Just do it as a favour for me. Go see her and I owe you one. I have to run, go talk to her today." Jessica hung up and trusted that her sister would at least go and check on Mabel for her.

Janice looked at the clock. It was three o'clock in the afternoon. Jessica must be really worried about her friend to get up early to call her. Without children and any family obligation, she knew her sister never rose before 9 a.m. George had just woke up from his nap. She sighed and started to gather things for their outing. Between staying home and waiting for another round of attack from Barbara, or going back to her own village to have a chat with her childhood friend - being nosy or not, she picked the latter.

***

Susan looked at the projected profit on the bottom line of her spreadsheet again. She thought she was mistaken at first glance, so she enlarged the display and counted the number of figures before the decimal point in front of her eyes. The figure was astonishing. It would be enough to set her family firm at another level if they go ahead with the deal. One of their biggest goals of the business was to launch an IPO, and Susan believed this would be the project to get them there. She was approached about a week ago, soon after the celebration of their recent success in business that they closed the deal with the second-largest property developer in the city to build a luxurious housing complex from the lands they'd acquired from Patrick Lee's mistresses and their children. They were disappointed that the biggest developer withdrew at the last minute. Hence, she was most intrigued when they knocked on her door again within such a short period of time.

Susan recalled her meeting with Cliffton, her counterpart from the richest and most powerful real estate developer in town:

Susan, this will be our flagship and pioneer project in the countryside. With the Government's participation and support, we believe your company will get much positive exposure to the public. It is the biggest endorsement you can get. We know very well that your father has been waiting for years for a good moment to launch your IPO. This is it, our collaboration will guarantee you a great response, as well as a prosperous future to come.

She looked at the map and the 3D simulation of the development again. Not only did the architecture looked prestigious, but only eco-sustainable houses would be built on the plot. Their partner was going to work with companies from Science Park and install the latest solar panels, for optimal efficiency on each house's rooftop and around the complex. They estimated the energy generated would satisfy most of the residents' need. Hydroponics would also be integrated into residential facilities such as the leisure clubhouse, swimming pool, etc. Only electric vehicles would be allowed in. This was going to be the most inspiring housing development ever planned in Hong Kong.

The only, and the biggest problem, was that the project was going to alter the landscape of Ma's village forever - and for the very worst. Susan knew very well that it would spark a fierce debate among herself, Sarah, Anthony and her father, Jimmy. And there would be infinite obstacles to overcome. Susan decided that, if she wanted to win, she would have to make her moves cautiously, and quietly.

***

Janice pushed open the gate of the house where Kenneth and Mabel lived with his parents and three daughters. Their two-story house occupied two plots of land, and several years ago, they got permission to build another house which they leased out to a family who moved to the countryside from the city. Kenneth fenced up the majority of the outdoor area to his tenant's side to push up the rent. As a result, their already little house was now squeezed in between two houses with only an alley between the front gate and the front door of the house. There was overgrown bamboo on both sides of the path leading to the house. Janice shielded George's head while she pushed the bamboo away one by one.

"Ouch!" Janice felt a scratch on her arm, and by the time she got up onto the front step of the door, she was shocked to find her arms covered with redness and scratch marks. Mabel rushed to the door after hearing someone's scream and was surprised to find Janice standing on the front doorstep, with her baby boy.

"Hi, Mabel, Jessica told me what happened, how horrible…" Janice had been figuring out what to say to Mabel on her drive over. She didn't think Mabel should fuss over the miscarriage too much - it was just a hiccup in the role of a village wife. She herself, and so should Mabel, know very well the reality - that you should keep trying and trying to give birth to as many boys as your female body could until menopause. Their worth was not counted with how well you took care of their families, but rather by the number of heirs to the land they could produce.

When Jessica begged her sister to be her representative to go comfort her childhood best friend, she did not pay attention to the fact that Janice would be bringing George with her, as she did everywhere she went, hence she did not anticipate the effect it would be on Mabel. Indeed, the last thing Mabel wanted to see was someone else's baby boy: another reminder of her failure to produce a male heir for her husband.

"How dare you?!" Mabel rushed back upstairs and left Janice standing there with her mouth wide open. Janice was shocked by both Mabel's reaction as well as her appearance. Mabel looked awful. Her hair was not combed, her eyes were red, and there was a big dark circle below each of her eyes. Despite being no longer pregnant, Mabel was as heavy and bloated as someone who was about to pop. *No wonder Kenneth would rather go for an artificial fertility treatment than touching his wife.*

Baby George screeched and gave out a piercing cry after being startled by his mum's screaming then with a strange woman shouting at him. Determined not to turn around and take the bamboo path again, Janice walked into the house and looked for the back door, which was common among the old village houses as it used to be used as the entrance and exit for the servants. Janice headed for the kitchen, knowing it's logically the way out from the back.

She heard waves of laughter of both men and women behind a door adjacent to the fridge. She pushed open the door and was surprised to find her brother there, with a lady dressed in very little that was close to indecent sitting on his lap, chatting away with Kenneth and two other young chaps she recognised from the village.

"Hey sis, go grab us four more beers from the fridge, please." Joe did not question why his sister was there. He was used to having women, many of them young and beautiful, run after him and answer to all his commands. Janice did not want to cause a scene at another's house, given she was pretty much trespassing now. Plus, she rarely heard the word, 'please,' from Joe. She sighed and took out four bottles of beers before heading out to the backyard.

Thanks to Janice's previous life as a career real estate agent, she learnt to put on a professional face with people from all walks of life as needed to facilitate her trade. She could be very smooth when she wanted to, although she did not do the footwork herself anymore. She'd hired a manager and a few staff to run the agency for her. Yet, she ran all the important relationships with the landlords, namely men like those in front of her, such that her employees, who had been employed from out of the village, would not be able to steal her businesses and clients from her.

Janice took a deep breath and put on her 'game face.'

"Hi, guys, what's the party for today?"

"Your baby brother's got a new girlfriend. We are helping him to welcome her and a few of her veeeeery charming friends to our village."

Janice was disgusted by how shamelessly Kenneth had his arm over another young girl's shoulders while his wife, who had just recently had a miscarriage, was crying upstairs. Yet, she reminded herself that there was nothing she could do that would change any of their behaviours. She wanted to flee the scene as soon as possible.

However, she was also not going to waste the effort she took to come all the way over and being molested by the wilderness outside the house. Before she left, she checked with everyone's properties status, and whether they would like to sell or get a new tenant in the foreseeable future. She took notes of everything and did a mental calculation. It's going to be a good year for her real estate business.

CHAPTER NINE

"Going to the library again?" Helen called after Joanne when she saw her carrying her backpack walking out of the house. "Go somewhere afterwards and meet some boys. Don't rush home for dinner!"

How ironic, Joanne thought to herself. Less than a decade ago, her parents used to lock her up in her room, with padlocks on both her door and windows, to make sure she did not sneak out to meet boys. These days she voluntarily locked herself up in her room whenever she wasn't working, and her mum took every chance she saw to encourage her to get out of the house to go 'meet boys.'

For years since the 'incident,' Joanne's most outgoing activities would be going to the main library in the city to bury herself in books. She always took the same outdoor sports backpack to bring the books she borrowed from the library home, so these days whenever she went out, she just brought the bag along as a habit. She felt protected with the straps wrapping around her that her mother was not going to pry on her, and whereabouts she was heading.

She was initially consumed by guilt about the abortion. She wanted to keep the baby she'd made with someone she truly loved. The father of the baby did not make much money, she believed they could have handled that. She had already started working on the family's books by then, and she was aware of how wealthy her family was. She had never imagined that her baby would be killed by its own grandparents. And they did not only kill her baby, the unlicensed doctor her father dragged her to did a nasty job on her womb. She was made sterile for life.

Years on, her guilt turned to rage. She was never able to forgive her parents. She thought of hurting herself but was luckily stopped by her cousin Susan. Susan was several years older than her, and she used to follow her cousin around when she was a little girl. Susan caught her when she was about to jump off a cliff near their great grandfather's gravestone. Susan comforted her when she sobbed for hours on the hill. She broke the news to her that with today's technology, she could have her eggs harvested and pay for a surrogate to carry the baby for her.

"You can still have your baby, but without the fat that comes with the pregnancy."

Joanne smiled for the first time since she told her mother about the little life growing in her tummy.

Life returned to normal at the bottom of the hill - Susan and Joanne had formed a solid bond and had become allies. Susan detested her uncle and aunt for doing something so barbarian to their daughter. She rarely went to the village events ever since then, and often blamed how she was caught up with something urgent that just popped up in the office. She was grateful that she saved Joanne's life years ago.

Joanne wanted to leave the village and the city forever, but Susan managed to convince her to stay and save up money before leaving for good. She rang Joanne up to invite her to go for a coffee. She wanted to present to her an opportunity to make some big bucks, at last, that would set her free while at the same time, make her families pay for the horrible deed they did to her.

***

Jaguar held his saw in position. The saw kissed the trunk of the tree, and the wood only gave in a little. Jaguar thought his primary evaluation was right - he would need the saw from the garage to take this banyan tree down. He had no choice but to remove this hundred years old tree that the villagers worshipped, otherwise the machinery could not pass through to get to the piece of land that he had been commissioned to build a house on. Jaguar would usually send his team of janitors to clear overgrown weeds and shrubs to make room for a path or for building purposes. However, when it came to trees, he would do it himself.

He believed that the trees were part of the family's lineage. So, if they had to go, he'd rather be the one bringing down the axe. Jaguar was a man of traditions. He had respect for everything that had been passed down to his generation. He would send his wife to the village temple before taking down every tree, to seek permission and blessings from his ancestors. After the ritual at the temple, the preparation would begin early the next morning.

One of his staff helped him replenish the petrol to run the chainsaw after he had picked out a couple from experience, that would be just right to fall the tree he intended to. Jaguar would then spend the morning, often with another staff tagged along, to study how to orchestra the felling, such that the trunk and branches of the tree would fall in the right spots, and not on another house, nor on a major path.

Thankfully, he ran a construction business and had all the tools he needed to carry out the operation. He had ladders of various heights and widths, which came in handy when he needed to pick one just right for a particular tree trunk. There were times that Jaguar would make a bet with his staff to choose the ladder that could lie flat on the cylindrical trunk. The losing one would have to haul all the ladders and chainsaws back to the company's warehouse. By the time all the physics had been studied, and tools were selected, it would be lunchtime. Jaguar would go for lunch and back to the office to clear his desk. Then after tea time, he and his team would head back to the tree cutting spot to do the actual cutting, which would last for less than an hour. If in the unfortunate case that Jaguar got all the calculations wrong, they would have to return the next day and follow the exact procedures to determine how the tree could be cut down. In direct contrast to what his wife Helen thought that cutting trees down was therapeutic for him, Jaguar saw it as another obligation that he, as the village chief, had to fulfil.

Jaguar envied his twin brother Jimmy. He was very proud of him for what he had achieved without the hand down from the family. He was conscious that everything he had, he owed to the fact that he was born the first boy in the family. Contrary to everyone's opinion, he did not regard himself as lucky. There were days he was so overwhelmed by the tasks he was born with that he wished he could swap places with Jimmy, or Jake. His fortune and power came with responsibilities.

When he was little, he spent more time with his grandfather, Jackson's father, than his own father. His grandfather, Jack, was highly regarded in the village. Jaguar used to tag along with Jack wherever he went, to help this relative with some life and death matter, to resolve disputes between villagers. Jack was a superhero in Jaguar's eyes, and he aspired to be like his grandfather one day when he became the chief of his village. His own father, Jackson, had no interest in taking on such a role. His passion laid within words and his paintbrushes. He passed the torch on to Jaguar the day he had his own family.

As the years went by, Jaguar realised that it was not easy and not at all glorious, trying to be everyone's hero. He felt the weight on his shoulders getting heavier by the day. Most of the villagers relied on him for employment, fighting for their rights on all aspects. Even when a relative cheated on his wife, he would find the wife at his doorsteps in tears, begging him to intervene. He felt the weight getting heavier and heavier. Then one day, it's become his duty to keep everyone fed, warm, happy, and the whole village in harmony.

In recent years, he had also been consumed by guilt. Guilt towards his children for not having played a major role in their upbringing, before he realised they had all grown up without him paying much attention to them. Among his six children, his first and second daughters were professionals, a lawyer and an accountant. Jacqueline was respected in and out of the village. He wondered if his eldest knew how proud he was of her. Joanne was a meticulous accountant who served the family well. His only regret was he and Helen had been too harsh on her over the 'incident' a long time ago - she had been hiding in the cocoon of her bedroom ever since. He made a silent promise to his second eldest that, if needed, he would protect her and financially support her for as long as he lived and beyond, should she never able to find a husband.

Janice, his third, was always lively and sassy. She did well with her cosy real estate business. He knew that out of respect for him, the villagers would give her their businesses. Jaguar was never worried about this child as she was very street smart. Janice was now married to an established family in the next village. She would be spoilt for the rest of her life.

Jessica, the youngest daughter, didn't he always have a soft spot for his lucky charm? The year she was born, not only did Helen fall pregnant with his first son pretty much right after her birth, he won the bid for a big building contract of a government project which led to many more for the years to come.

He sighed when he thought of his sons. After years yearning for a male heir, they finally had Joe and Jay. Although he often put the blame on Helen, he understood he could not shy away from the responsibility that he, as their father, had an important role to play for their upbringings. He was still clueless about how Jay ended up liking boys. His sexual orientation had put his parents into an even more difficult position to have any influence on Joe.

Joe was now their last hope to continue their name and bloodline. He was clueless about what to do with this boy. Approaching thirty, Joe showed no signs of settling down. He loved chasing girls with fast and fancy sports cars. Despite being privileged and extremely spoilt, Joe was no fool. He could charm when he needed to, especially with his mother. He could talk his way out of troubles. Jaguar still remembered how Joe convinced a Kiosk owner not to call the police nor tell his parents after being caught stealing candies from the jars. The story was only relayed back to him later, as praise of how quick-witted Joe was!

Once he turned the saw off, Jaguar heard a group of people talking in the distance, with cameras and clipboards in their hands. Every now and then, there would be government officers visiting the village, to check on the utility infrastructure, to evaluate the potential of telecom facilities expansion.

This group, however, looked somehow peculiar to Jaguar. He gave himself a quick wipe and dusted the wood debris off his trousers. He approached the party and introduced himself as the village chief and enquired what survey this group of four was conducting.

The leading guy greeted Jaguar with a genuine-looking smile. He handed his name card respectfully to Jaguar. Jaguar inspected the card closely. It said Benny Lau, who was a civil engineer. Benny explained to Jaguar that his firm had been appointed by the Government to do routine testing of soil quality. They then would submit the data to the concerned departments to assist in their evaluation of the safety of the slopes around the village as well as the stability of the local trees.

Jaguar shook his head. When had he become so sensitive and suspicious? He must be getting old. There were days like today when Jaguar felt his life was overpowered by confusion, obligations, and stress, and he was grateful that there was one place on earth where he could seek comfort.

Chapter Ten

Jaguar inserted his key into the front door of a two-bedroom apartment he'd purchased about five years ago. He could hear the sweet singing voice of Tanya coming from the kitchen where it was enveloped with the aroma of his favourite dishes. He wrapped his arms around Tanya from behind and gave her a peck on the cheek. Tanya squealed with delight at the sight of her lover. She quickly turned the hobs off and asked Jaguar if he would like anything to drink.

"Yes, I would like to drink all your juices…" Jaguar whispered into Tanya's ears while he cupped her in between her groins. Tanya let out a moan, and Jaguar swiftly swept her off her feet. He carried her into the master bedroom. Although he knew well that Tanya had already settled her eighty-year-old mother into the care home for the day, he habitually kicked the door closed to ensure some privacy before sinking into the bed with his mistress.

***

Jaguar would have never dreamt about being unfaithful to his wife. Tanya came into his life about eight years ago when she joined his construction company as an administrative officer. She was hired by his office manager. Tanya was not particularly beautiful, but she had this innocence and grace in her that appealed very much to him.

He remembered very well the day he met Tanya for the first time. He was so enchanted by this young lady that he adjusted the blind in his office and watched Tanya the whole day from the inside of his room. Jaguar called in his office manager and questioned her decision on hiring an outsider to the company, contrary to the usual practice.

"Tanya is a nice girl, boss. She's the niece of an extended family of mine in the city. Poor girl, her father has recently passed away. Her mother hasn't been the same ever since. She needs to be taken care of. She can only afford to rent a one-bedroom apartment in the suburbs. It's actually closer to us and gives her a big saving on transportation costs in her commute than getting a job in the city. You will see, boss. Tanya is very hardworking and a quick learner. And she has a university degree! You know very well that Betsy is getting married next month and won't be with us anymore. We had to find her replacement to cope with all the new jobs we have on hand…"

Indeed, Jaguar agreed that Tanya was a diligent worker. She was organised and impeccable with her assignments. She developed a new system for the whole team, which made everyone's work much more efficient than before. Moreover, Tanya was soft-spoken and kind. Jaguar found himself spending more time in the office, much more than he needed to, because of the new hire.

Soon Helen caught wind of the new girl in the office who was loved by everybody. She decided to drop by one day to say hello and welcome her in person. She prided herself as a pillar standing behind her husband and treated his employees as families. Her visit to the office caught everyone by surprise, including both Tanya and her husband. She caught them looking at each other for a bit too long to be just an employer and an employee. Helen pretended she did not see anything. However, before the end of the week, Tanya was sent packing and was no longer seen in the office. Jaguar was outraged and called his office manager into his office.

"Explain to me why Tanya was fired! I thought she's been marvellous at her work?" Jaguar demanded an answer to why his favourite employee had been let go.

"I am so sorry boss. I thought Tanya was a great girl, too. I did not know that she's that desperate with money. Mrs Ma caught her one lunch break that she was going to take money from the petty cash box. Please forgive me, boss, I did not mean to bring a thief into the office. I had promised Mrs Ma that I would never hire an outsider again."

Jaguar hit his fist on his desk and made his office manager jump. "Get out - now!"

His office manager took the cue and fled from the village chief's office, regretting ever helping her relative. Little did she know that her boss was angry with his wife for firing Tanya out of jealousy. He was certain Tanya did not do anything to deserve such treatment. Besides, Jaguar knew very well that the petty cash in the office was never more than a few hundred dollars. Helen must have become suspicious of something after her recent visits to the office – but nothing had happened between Jaguar and Tanya. It was all very innocent. They'd only exchanged a tender look here and there, and there was the lingering of their fingers on each other for a bit too long when he helped Tanya with some heavy samples of construction materials. Yet, all these small gestures had made Jaguar feel like a young chap all over again. Without himself realising it, the new girl in the office had gradually captured his heart.

When everyone was out during lunch break, he looked for the large binder that carried all the staff records.

Luckily, Tanya's was still there. He quickly noted down her address, contact number, and returned the binder to its place. That afternoon, he acted as nothing had happened.

His office manager sighed a huge relief that the village chief had forgiven her. *No more outsider*, she reminded herself again.

Jaguar rang the bell of the address stated on Tanya's employee record. He prayed that Tanya was home as he did not have all day. He told Helen that he was going into the city to check on the retail prices of the latest construction materials to study the potential increase in the margin of their related business. He did not call Tanya's number in advance, either. He had no clue what to say to her. They did not have much of verbal interactions in the office anyway. He did not want to scare her away before he had the chance to look her in the eyes again.

Tanya was surprised to hear a few sturdy knocks on the door. She and her mother rarely had visitors, and they had only recently moved to this new address. None of her friends nor distant families were aware of their whereabouts these days. She opened the door and found herself frozen for a few moments. She was speechless to find her previous employer standing in front of her.

"Who's that Tanya?" Tanya's seventy-three-year-old mother could not hear clearly, and her eyesight was blurry, too, but she could make out a large man standing at the door.

"No one, mum, just a colleague from my previous company. He helped bring something I had forgotten." Tanya quickly came up with a story, seeing Jaguar carrying a bag in his hand. She invited Jaguar in and cleared the objects on the two-seaters that took up most of the space of the living area.

"What a lost head you are! Don't forget to invite your friend for a cup of tea before he goes, after he comes all the way here to see us," Tanya's mum shouted as she could hardly hear herself.

"Yes, mum. It's time for your nap. Let me help you to your bed first."

Jaguar stole a glimpse of the only bedroom before he could stop himself. His heart felt sour when he took in her living conditions. She and her mother shared a bunk bed; her mother slept on the lower bunk, which he saw Tanya helping into the bed for her afternoon nap. He assumed Tanya must be sleeping above her mother. Besides the bed, the bedroom was only big enough for a closet. The apartment lounge was about the size of the foyer of his house back in the Ma village. He guessed the sofa must be brought from their old place as it looked out of place in its tiny surroundings. There was a small corner table at one end of the sofa and a folded table leaning on the wall at the other end. There was a large TV unit facing the sofa which Jaguar noticed had been used as the main storage of the house. There was a twenty-two inch TV - the most luxurious item in the house, Jaguar suspected. The rest of the furniture was filled with all sorts of items, books, rolls of toilet paper, biscuits, rice, fruits, etc.

When Tanya came back out after settling her mother, she and Jaguar looked at each other for a long time. At first, the silence was awkward. Jaguar took out some cakes from inside the hold-all he was carrying. He offered Tanya one. Tanya stood up and offered to make some tea. Jaguar grabbed her hand and stop her. Tanya turned around and stared at him in the eyes. Suddenly, neither of them could stand the tension that had been built up over the past weeks between them. Jaguar pulled Tanya over and took her mouth in, and kissed her for the longest time he could remember kissing anyone. They quickly undressed each other and made love on the giant looking two-seater in the tiny living room.

***

Despite the twenty years' difference in age, Jaguar and Tanya never seemed to be able to get their hands off each other. Ever since that afternoon, Jaguar visited Tanya once a week. He made an excuse to Helen that it was his market visit day. He mixed in a few things to make it impossible for Helen to track where he went. One week he could be at a new housing development to study the new layout. The week after could be meeting with a few retailers to see if he could become their wholesalers since his business acquired tonnes and tonnes of building materials. He always reminded himself to spend an hour at a site so he would smell just like coming back from work when he got home to Helen. Thanks to the fact that Tanya had worked at the office before and knew the inside out of the operation, she would have done the footwork for Jaguar so they could maximise their time together. Tanya was so good at her 'job' that Jaguar's business actually benefited from the new ventures efficiently executed by his mistress.

Jaguar soon found out from Tanya that Helen had lied and bad-mouthed Tanya that she had committed theft, which left her no choice but to terminate her. The reason which Helen gave Tanya to let her go was by hiring an outsider into the firm, it undermined Jaguar's reputation and credibility as the village chief. Tanya bought the lie told by the wife of her boss who she had a massive crush on, packed her things and left before anyone returned from lunch break.

Jaguar had proposed to help Tanya and her mother to move to a more spacious apartment right from the start. Tanya insisted on being self-dependent and refused any materialistic return from her former employer, that was until the time Jaguar injured his back due to the lack of space to manoeuver when they were together, so she reluctantly agreed to let Jaguar subsidise her rent and move to a larger flat.

Two years later, the side jobs that Tanya did for Jaguar brought him a significant increase in the number of clients and profits. Jaguar convinced Tanya to take a share of the fruits brought to him from her works. He purchased a modest apartment to be put under Tanya's name. It was nothing grand but comfortable enough for Tanya and her mother. The apartment building was also close to an elderly day care home that Tanya's mother started to spend a few days a week at. There she had a regular medical check-up, she made new friends, and there were staff and volunteers teach her crafts and singing. Her condition had much improved ever since. Tanya was grateful for how kind Jaguar had been to her. Before long, Jaguar and Tanya were head over heels in love with each other. Tanya's humble apartment had become a refuge for Jaguar, whenever he felt confused, frustrated, disappointed, and wanted to seek comfort from someone who had totally earned his trust and lust.

"I think you should go to Jay's wedding, even if you don't approve of same-sex marriage," Tanya spoke to Jaguar softly after they'd made love to each other.

"Not you, too. Where am I going to hide my face after I come back from a gay wedding?" Jaguar would never raise his voice at Tanya as she rarely disagreed with him nor questioned his judgement. She always found a sideways approach to persuade Jaguar about anything.

"Yes, especially me. Love is blind. Look at us. I am of the same age as your elder daughters. If over twenty years of age difference meant nothing when it came to our love, maybe gender meant little to Jay and his fiancée."

"I just find it disgusting when I imagine a man with another man…"

"I am sure others would think the same about us… Go as a display of support and love for your son. You do not have to support gay marriage; you just need to be there for him. No one will think any less of you because you go to your son's wedding, same-sex or not. Else do it for me; you won't be able to make me an honest woman, but go to your son's wedding to honour our unconventional love." Tanya sounded very firm. Jaguar was touched by how she fought for his son - who had no idea about her existence.

Chapter Eleven

"I am heartbroken to see you go, Chi Kin. I almost wanted to injure my other leg, so you will come to help me again. But you did an excellent job to get me back on my feet in 3 weeks!" Grandma Rose was sad to see Chi Kin go. She thought she was going to be miserable having to do all the physiotherapies her doctor had ordered - she did not expect that doing exercises could be so much fun.

As she had recovered a week sooner than the recovery programme planned, Rose asked Chi Kin to come up with some fitness exercise suitable for her age and level. She invited a dozen villagers to come to join the class. It was fun, and Rose and her friends often ended bent over backwards by laughing too much. The other grandmas had also come to love this young man, who was kind, respectful, and at the same time hilarious. He flirted with the ladies mercilessly, and the grandmas returned the gesture in kind. Everyone was sad to hear the classes had come to an end and wanted to conspire a scheme to keep Chi Kin in the village.

"Grandma, maybe I can help." Jay's idea had worked, and Chi Kin had successfully captured Grandma Rose's heart. Although he had not anticipated the plan would go so well that Grandma Rose was genuinely upset when the physiotherapies came to an end.

"I have proposed to Chi Kin so he would become your grandchild, too."

"Wahahahaha, I forgot I have another good grandchild - you. You are a good boy, Jay, making a joke to cheer grandma up." Grandma Rose chuckled at such idea, only she found a couple of minutes later, her youngest grandchild was still staring at her, this time with a pleading look.

"Oh, mercy my Goddess of Compassion," realisations dawned on Rose. "How come I did not manage to put two and two together?" Grandma Rose covered her face and could not believe that it was Chi Kin, who had schemed up with her grandchild to win her heart and approval.

"I am so sorry, Grandma. We did not mean to deceive you. But we have no choice as this was the only way for you to get to know Chi Kin. Even if we can't get your blessing, at least you have now recovered and know that I am going to spend the rest of my life with a great man…" Jay found himself shrinking again in front of his favourite Grandma Rose.

"No, I am the one who should apologise. You should not have to go through all that to get my support. But you were right, it was the only way to make us see the love of your life without prejudice. Grandma is not as open-minded as your grandpa, but I am not an unprogressive old rag. Do you think Grandma Rose is not aware that we live in a different era now? Although I have to say it was a splendid effort to get grandma's approval, and Chi Kin has absolutely earned it." Rose was slightly ashamed of the length that the two young men had gone through to seek her vote.

"Do you really mean it, Grandma? Does it mean that you are going to talk to Dad for me?" Jay jumped and gave his grandma a bear hug.

"So, your Grandma Rose is only your means to a goal - your Dad is your holy grail, isn't he? I can't promise you I can talk some sense into that stubborn head of your father's, but I will try, I promise I will try…"

***

"Does Uncle Jimmy know about this?" Joanne asked Susan.

"No, and no. My father had no knowledge about this project nor our collaboration," Susan assured Joanne. She held her breath and waited for Joanne's response. She knew that Joanne's participation was key to the success of what she had in plan.

"If I say 'yes,' how much are you willing to pay me? You know very well that I can no longer stay in the family if Dad finds out about this." Joanne emphasised the seriousness to her cousin about what she was about to get herself into - a no way back deal with the devil and her forever betrayal to her family.

"Fifty million Hong Kong dollars. That will be more than enough for you to set yourself up nicely where you want to go and pay for all the fertility treatments for you to have children in future."

That will be more enough, Joanne thought to herself. Just ten per cent of that sum would allow her to buy a house in that little town in Portugal. She had done her research over the years - fertility treatments in Spain, the neighbouring country, were very affordable compared to other main cities around the world. She could live comfortably with the rest of the money for the rest of her life, and probably her children's lives, too.

"What will I have to do to earn that?" Joanne looked into Susan's eyes and hoped that she did not have to kill anyone to realise the dream that had been keeping her hope up for the last decade.

"Not much, indeed. All you have to do is to share with us the accounts of the villagers, especially on those whose lands we are interested in. We need to know the price we need to offer, enough to make them say yes but not too much that would eat into our profit."

"That's it?" Joanne somehow felt there was still a catch in the deal that her cousin offered her because it sounded too good to be true.

"There is one more thing." Susan unrolled some maps that Joanne recognised were those on the vast area of the Ma village. "This, this, this, and this building are keys to winning our tender. These properties are under the holding of a limited company in which you are the Director. Our real estate partner will compensate for the sale of these buildings, but we need you to sign over and facilitate the transaction. Of course, no one needs to know anything until our development is ready to commence works. By then, you will be long gone from home." Susan assured Joanne while she tried to look for the facial expression on Joanne's face for her reaction.

Joanne gasped, listening to Susan telling her what she had to do in order to earn her peace she had been yearning for years.

"That will set you free from home AND make them pay for all the horrible things they did to you, in the name of the stupid honour, all those years ago," Susan reminded her cousin while her own palms started to sweat. She needed Joanne to be her ally - or her partner in crime, in this case - to close the deal of the century, as well as the opportunity to get her company into the exchange market.

"Can I think about it? I won't tell a soul, I promise. I just need to process everything." Joanne needed to think it over, to make sure that's what she wanted, and not just some impulsive decision made out of anger.

"Of course, but we don't have much time. I need your answer before the end of the week." Susan stood up and left the library, leaving Joanne to ponder her offer in the privacy of the deserted reference library room.

***

"I'm pregnant," Joanne told Christian nervously, not knowing what to do with the baby she just found out that had been growing in her womb for the past three months. She only realised she was at least two months late a couple of days ago. She travelled to town to get a pregnancy test kit from a pharmacy. She was more than frightened to see the double line on the little window showing the result. She bought an international calling card from a convenience store, dialled the number she had memorised and demanded to see her secret boyfriend as soon as possible.

Joanne met her lover Christian during an academic exchange programme. It was only a week of study at the sister college in Macau of the university she was attending, but those few days altered Joanne's story for the rest of her life. Christian was a second-generation Portuguese, and he was an assistant professor in the same department where Joanne went to. Christian had been assigned to look after the students from Hong Kong. It was love at first sight and knowing they only had a week with each other, Christian asked Joanne out on the second day. They went out in secret, and Christian showed Joanne his passion as well as all the beautiful sights and the romantic colonial spots in the city. Before the end of the exchange programme, Christian and Joanne had become love birds and were completely crazy about one another. With two cities only about an hour of ferry journey away from each other, Christian came to Hong Kong often to see his girlfriend. Everything was done in secret. Joanne's parents were never suspicious as they rarely paid attention to their second daughter and assumed she spent most of her time off school at the library.

"Let's get married and you move to Macau with me. I will look after you and the baby. I don't make much money now, but I will become a professor in a few years, then things will be much more comfortable." Contrary to Joanne's worries, Christian was excited about the idea of becoming a father. He's going to turn thirty soon and felt it was about time to start his own family.

Joanne was relieved as well as touched by Christian's reaction to the news. They began to talk about their future and what name they were going to give to their baby if it's a boy or if it's a girl. Christian was ready to go and ask Jaguar for his daughter's hand; however, Joanne told him to wait for her to break the news to her parents first.

"They are very traditional, especially where we come from and the fact that you are not Chinese." The more Joanne thought about it, the more nervous she got. She was almost certain her father was going to be outraged and want to beat the hell out of Christian for knocking his daughter up. She had the responsibility to protect her baby's father now, and she cursed herself for being clouded by the excitement from Christian's proposal and almost overlooking the sensitivity of her situation.

"If mum and dad are not too mad, we can have the baby first then plan about the wedding. Mind you, the banquet is going to be big, and it has to be in our village. My father is the village chief so there is no chance we can escape from that. But if dad is angry, we will have to speed everything up and get married as soon as possible."

Christian was used to the culture in the Far East, growing up among both Chinese and Portuguese in Macau.

He was happy to go with the flow and whatever would make Joanne happy.

Joanne found a quiet afternoon to break the news to her parents. She was not too worried. Christian was a fine gentleman, and he had a good job. She could be a bit young to become a mother at the age of twenty - but so did her mother.

While she expected her parents would be a bit crossed that she got pregnant before the wedding, she had never in her wildest imagination pictured how Helen and Jaguar reacted. Jaguar lost his temper and broke a dining chair when he swore he was going to break the baby's father's leg as he did with the furniture. Helen told her she had put shame onto herself as well as her family. She must not give birth to the baby. She insisted that she had to go for an abortion; otherwise, no one would ever be going to marry her.

"We always thought you were a good girl, and only went to the library to study after school. Turns out you are a whore who sleeps around and gets yourself pregnant!" Jaguar fired his palm onto Joanne's head and demanded she tells him who the father was. Realising the graveness of the situation and the threat to Christian, Joanne bit her lips and told her mum that she was not sure who the father was. Her answer drove Jaguar's rage through the roof. He locked Joanne in her room and forbade her to come out without his permission.

Locked in her own room, Joanne trembled. She was scared and felt sick to her stomach, worried that her parents were going to find out about Christian and cause him harm.

***

The next evening her mother brought Joanne some soup. She felt a migraine soon after and passed out. When she woke up, she found herself lying on a hospital bed. She felt a stabbing pain in her tummy. Panic washed over her body. She saw a middle-aged man wearing a surgical cap talking to her father.

"The foetus is out. It was supposed to be a baby boy. She's still young. She should be able to recover pretty quickly, in a week or two."

Upon hearing what the 'doctor' said to her father, realisation dawned on Joanne. Her mother had drugged her, and they had brought her to this shabby looking clinic to force an abortion on her. Her baby was gone; her baby boy was gone. She screamed and screamed. The next thing she knew was a few pairs of hands pressing her down, followed by a needle into her vein. Then everything went black.

CHAPTER TWELVE

Tears streamed down Joanne's face. She barely survived the infection she had had in the past two weeks. The unlicensed doctor whose expertise was to carry out illegal abortions did a lousy job on her. Joanne started to have fever and hallucinations several days after her parents brought her back home. Her parents locked her up as a punishment and only left a tray of food twice a day outside her door. After a day of untouched food, Helen went into Joanne's room to check on her daughter, only to find her burning body shivering in a pool of sweat. She could have died if she was not sent to the hospital in time. The infection in her womb was horrendous.

Jaguar refused to tell the doctor what had happened, and because of Jaguar's close relationship with the local police in the countryside, he escaped from the possible charges. Nevertheless, the doctor had made it clear that whoever did the butcher job on Joanne had to be responsible for the fact that Joanne had been made sterile for the rest of her life. Joanne overheard her parents arguing, and Helen blamed Jaguar for rushing the doctor when he did the operation, worrying that the drug to put her asleep was going to wear off at any time.

Besides the pain and heartbreaks, Joanne was eager to get in touch with Christian. She was supposed to call him as soon as she told her parents that she was pregnant and was going to be married to the father of the baby. No one had expected such a turn of events. She had been grounded and was forbidden to use the phone. It had been weeks, and Joanne imagined how restless and worried Christian must have become because of the lack of news from her.

After learning about what happened from Jacqueline, Susan was furious about what her aunt and uncle did to her cousin. She went to visit Joanne and was heartbroken seeing the state she was in. Susan asked Joanne if there was anything she could do to help. Joanne poured her heart out to Susan and begged her to pass on a message to Christian for her.

"Call this number and tell him that I am alright as soon as possible. He must be worried sick. Can you come back tomorrow? I will write him a letter, and you can help me post it?"

Susan looked at her cousin, whose sunken eyes pleaded with her. She nodded her head and said she would help her to communicate with her boyfriend.

"Don't tell him about what actually happened. I don't want him to do anything stupid. I am going to tell him that I miscarried. As soon as mum lets me out of the house again, I will go find him."

Thanks to Susan, who also stopped her in time from doing something stupid herself, Joanne was back in her secret relationship with Christian again. Helen let her out and about again five months after the 'incident,' positive that her daughter had learnt her lesson. Joanne only hung out with Susan or went to the library during those days, in order not to raise suspicions from her parents. Joanne would go to Susan's office and use her computer to write emails to Christian, and they would make a date and meet up in the library which she told her mother was where she studied for her exams. Susan always covered up for her whenever she needed some privacy with her boyfriend. Christian was sad that Joanne had miscarried their baby but believed that she was still young and they could have more in the future. There were many occasions when Joanne wanted to break the news to Christian that she could no longer bear him any children, but she could not bring herself to do that whenever she was about to open her mouth.

***

Things were going well. Christian finally became a professor and Joanne had got her qualification as an accountant. They had a whole future ahead of them, only to be ruined by the discovery that Christian had been diagnosed with terminal prostate cancer. There had been little symptoms, and whatever Christian had, he dismissed them as stress from working towards his professorship. He was also too young to get such cancer, they believed.

Nevertheless, cancer took Christian's life away in such a short time that Joanne did not see it coming at all. Susan orchestrated a getaway trip, and Joanne managed to spend the last days with the love of her life. Christian's dying wish was to have his ashes buried in a little town in Portugal where his parents grew up in. Joanne made her promise and kissed her lover goodbye. She brought Christian's ashes back and hid in her room, along with a heavy heart. She locked herself in most of the time ever since.

***

"Susan, I'll do it." Joanne quickly hung up the phone, worried that she would change her mind if she did not. The past few days, her love story and tragedy had been playing in her head in loops like a movie. She had to honour the dying wish of Christian, and take revenge on those who had ripped away her lover and their unborn baby, as well as happiness from her life.

Chapter Thirteen

Jessica stepped out of Santa Barbara Airport and welcomed the warm and dry breeze caressing the skin of her face. It was nice not having to wear a heavy cardigan for a change. The weather in London had been funny in the past two months. It was either roasting hot when a heatwave was hitting Western Europe, or damp and cold. She had been looking forward to having some guaranteed sunshine and mild temperatures across the continent. In fact, she was excited about Jay's wedding. She was almost grateful that since he was gay, he had to have his wedding outside the village. She had never visited the West Coast of the U.S. Thanks to the fact that she was in London, the flight was much shorter than if she had to fly from Hong Kong.

Since Jay was not going to have many of the family attending his wedding, Jessica enjoyed a VIP reception. Jay had arranged an airport transfer for her. The driver had welcomed her earlier at the arrival hall, who was now diligently waiting for her to finish her cigarette before opening the passenger door of a limousine for her. For a moment, Jessica wished Joe was gay, too. She loved the fact that Jay was sweet and thoughtful. If it were a village wedding, she would have been expected to enslave herself around the kitchen as well as at the banquet.

As a lover of nature, Jessica was in awe when the car drove past the vast open space of hills, vineyards, and ocean. It was a different kind of nature she usually encountered. She had close-up interactions with plants and colours on a daily basis, but here, it was all zoomed out. Acres and acres of openness unfolded one by one as the car drove closer to her destination. Jessica took in a deep breath - the aroma of nature here differed from that in the UK as well as back home in Hong Kong. She wanted to imprint the scent in her head.

The limousine driver pulled over at a lodge that Jessica assumed was the office or reception of the campground she was going to stay at, and where Jay's wedding was going to take place. The vehicle looked totally out of place in the all-natural backdrop. The campground was nestled in the historic groves of oak and in the vicinity of a beach. Jay had briefed the guests about the natural surroundings of their destination wedding, which resembled glamping, or 'glamorous camping.'

Guests were put into either a luxury cabin or a yurt. As a solo guest, Jessica was thrilled to be assigned to a yurt. The yurt was a stand-alone structure built on a wooden platform. It was abundantly spacious for one person. There was a queen-size bed in the middle, with the addition of a closet, writing desk, and a daybed, and there was still room in the yurt to move around. Jessica's favourite part was its raised rooftop that included a domed skylight for easy stargazing from the comfort of her temporary home.

Jay suggested Jessica arrive a few days before the wedding so that she could have time to adjust to the jet-lag as well as enjoy what Napa Valley had to offer. After she had freshened up with a shower and a much-needed nap, Jessica biked from her yurt to the front office for visitors' information. Her heart swelled, taking in the scenery around her. She had a feeling that it's going to be a wonderful stay.

"Follow this route, and it will take your bike-ride through the national forest. After that, if you would still like to venture further, take this route and visit the llama farm. The gentleman there is about to leave for the same activity. He's also a guest at the wedding - see if you would like to go and watch out for each other," the young receptionist suggested to Jessica.

Jessica didn't pay attention to the arrival of other guests and was surprised to find someone standing at the corner, checking out the bulletin board. When the man turned to look at her after overhearing the receptionist's idea, Jessica gasped; she thought she was staring at a younger version of Idris Elba.

Idris Elba broke into a heart-melting smile and walked over to Jessica to introduce himself. "Lovely to meet you. I am Luke, a friend of the groom."

For a moment, Jessica thought she heard 'Luther,' but she composed herself and introduced herself as the sister of the groom.

"Which groom?" Jessica asked, and both of them laughed.

Within minutes, both Luke and Jessica took off on their respective bikes and headed towards the national forest. Luke told Jessica that he was originally from the UK, which explained his sexy English accent that confused Jessica along with his 'Luther' appearance. He was currently based in Paris at a client's site.

"I relocate every couple of years, depending on the location of the project we are working on. That's the perk of being a programmer, I can work anywhere in the world. On the downside, is that I have little certainty regarding where I will be in the medium term. I met Jay at a party when he came to Paris for work. I injured my leg earlier from a bike accident. Thanks to his fiancé Tony who'd joined him there for a holiday, I had two sessions of physiotherapy with him, and my leg was as good as new. They are very sweet to invite me to their wedding; this place is out of the world."

Jessica did a mental sigh. As soon as Luke mentioned he met Jay at a party, she knew that another incredibly handsome and sexy man had been snapped up by another man. Yet, she cheered herself up and tried to focus on the beauties surrounding her and the fact she was there for Jay's big day, not on a blind date with a random hot man.

Indeed, the pair had a blast. They cycled deep into the woods. They stopped by a natural waterfall. Both of them were drenched with sweat. Jessica stripped herself and went for a dip in the water, assuming a gay guy would not mind female nudity. Luke followed suit. Because of the mist from the waterfall, Jessica could hardly catch a glimpse of Luke's glorious body. She nudged herself again that Luke was already taken, by the other half of the world's population.

After cooling themselves off under the waterfall, they rode all the way to the llama farm in the north. They did a quick tour before the farm was closed for the day. Jessica bought a llama stuffed animal for George, a handful of cardigans for her family, and one for her flatmate.

When Luke and Jessica got back to the campground, they both felt exhausted but exhilarated. It had passed the European dinner time, and they agreed they needed the bed more than a meal. They wished each other goodnight and returned to their own yurts, which Jessica was delighted to find out were cosily located close to one another.

The next day Jessica and Jay had made a date to spend the day beautifying themselves at a luxurious spa resort half an hour away from where they were. Jay followed the tradition not to see the groom the day before the wedding ceremony. He was going to bunk up together with Jessica.

***

"So what do you think of Luke?" Jay asked Jessica as soon as their mani-pedi therapists had settled them down side by side at two pedicure lounge chairs.

"He is gorgeous, charming, and sexy as hell. And stop teasing me and trying to prove how hot you gay guys are." Jessica lifted her fingers off the soaking bowl and gave her baby brother a nudge on his arm.

"Ouch! Who told you that he's gay? Your considerate gay brother, me, remembered to invite some straight dudes so you can have a one night stand with. You are very welcome."

Jessica covered her mouth, completely shocked by the breaking news Jay just delivered. She then covered her face as she recalled embarrassingly how she took all her clothes off in front of Luke and walked the distance down to the waterfall.

Chapter Fourteen

"You didn't?!" Jay exclaimed and threw his head back to laugh.

"I did… bared all!" Jessica recounted how she'd stripped completely naked in front of Luke to have a dip in the waterfall during their bike ride in the national forest, assuming he was gay, as friends of both Jay and Tony.

"I did not think you as bold like this, sis. My hats off to you." Jay took his pretend tall hat off and bowed to Jessica. "Next time you see Luke, you can tell him, 'Now you have inspected the merchandise, it's time to take me to your yurt…'"

"Oh, shut up! Can you please find a way to tell him that the whole thing was a misunderstanding?"

"Tell him that you mistook him as gay? It's even more of an insult to a straight guy. I wouldn't if I were you, unless you aren't interested in him at all."

"Forget about it." Jessica's shoulders dropped out of frustration.

"Oh, you have a crush on Luke! Come on, sis, just go with the flow. You straight people are such sissies when it comes to flirting. You only have a few more days here to get him into your pants."

"Now that's an insult, to be called a sissy by a gay man. I am not that desperate." Jessica could not believe what her baby brother was suggesting to her.

"Look at your skin, you are so dry. I doubt you can remember the last time you went out on a date with anyone. We will get your face fixed later after our mani-pedi."

"It's none of your business. Although, I wouldn't mind having my face pampered, I totally deserve a heavenly facial if I have to endure you throughout your wedding." Jessica was going to be the maid of honour. She'd been one for her friends before, but it would be the first time for a gay couple.

***

Helen was turning her head left and right frantically to look for the taxi-stand signage at the Santa Barbara Airport.

"I told you we should have come with Jake. If we can't find this place, we are going to miss the wedding! It'll be your fault." Jaguar was furious with his wife. The wedding was going to take place that afternoon, and he had no idea where they were. He only knew he needed a shower and a shave badly if he wanted to look presentable when he walked his son down the aisle.

"I had to wait for my tailor to alter my dress. I am the mother of the groom, I have to wear a 'Kua.'" Helen insisted she had to put on her elaborate traditional Chinese wedding dress that was fully embroidered with pearls and sparkly sequins for the mother to showcase the family's wealth and status. She had put on some weight since Janice's wedding, and her tailor rushed the alteration within days when Jaguar changed his mind at last minute to attend Jay's wedding.

Thankfully, Helen found the taxi stand. The queue moved quickly and soon it was their turn. Helen used her limited English and pointed at the address Jake had written down for her. Jake had also kindly prepared another note for the reception at the wedding venue that they were to put in a cabin that he called in two days ago to reserve. The driver glanced at the paper and waved them onto the cab. Within minutes, they were on the way to join the wedding of their youngest son.

***

"Are you nervous, baby brother?" Jessica helped Jay to adjust his bowtie. The couple had done the traditional Chinese tea servings for their senior relatives in the morning. Tony's parents were there, while Jake and Jacqueline sat in for Jay's side of the family. Now they were getting ready for the big moment.

"Of course I am, I am going to vow to love and fuck the same person for the rest of my life," Jay sighed.

"It's still not too late to run, baby brother," Jessica teased.

"Well, somehow I am very pleased with Tony's glorious penis and…" Jay smiled to himself.

"Stop! Stop! Stop! I don't want to picture it." Jessica made a sweeping gesture to erase whatever had begun to arise in her head.

***

The guests had been seated on rows of chairs arranged neatly on a vast green field overlooking the ocean. The lumination was a romantic mix of pink and orange. The couple were going to exchange their vows at sunset. The back of the chairs were dressed in creamy silk ribbon with a bouquet of dried lavender tied in the middle. It was a sweet compliment to the boutonnieres the couple were wearing. Their boutonnieres were a single large white orchid, tied with a lavender colour ribbon, hand-crafted by Jessica, which she had already drawn the design in a portrait as a souvenir for her baby brother before leaving London.

A violinist and a cellist started playing. A lady sitting in the front row among the guests stood. She walked to a spot between the two string instrument performers, and started singing Etta James's 'At Last.' Everyone was bathed in the romance of the melodies and the meaningful lyrics of the song for the special union. When the music stopped, Tony and his father got ready at the beginning of the aisle. All the guests stood. Tony's father walked him down the aisle while being cheered by the guests on both sides. The duo stopped below the arch which was decorated with vines and adorable bubble fairy lights. Both grooms would be given away by their respective father figure.

Then it was Jay's turn. Uncle Jake offered his elbow and Jay hooked his arm in it. They walked down the aisle, and the guests gave them applauds. Then midway from the arch where Tony and his father were standing, Uncle Jake stopped and said to Jay, "My dear nephew, thanks for giving me the honour to walk you down half the aisle. But I think your father would like to be the one who gives you away."

Uncle Jake moved aside, and Jay found his father standing in front of him, looking at his smartest self Jay had ever seen him. He had shaved all the beard and stubbles off his face and was wearing a three-piece suit. Jaguar offered Jay his arm. Jay could hardly hold his tears. Never in his wildest dreams did he expect his father to turn up to his same-sex wedding. The guests took in everything, and there were no dry eyes at the audience.

At the end of the aisle, Jaguar gave Tony's father a firm handshake. He then went to shake Tony's hand and warned him to be nice to his son; otherwise, the hundreds of Ma's people back in the village would go after him. Jessica laughed at her father joke while dabbing her eyes. She, too, was surprised and touched by her parents' surprise appearance at the wedding.

Maybe there's hope in our family, she thought optimistically to herself.

After a simple but solemn ceremony when the couple exchanged their vows they wrote for each other, the celebrant pronounced Jay and Tony husband and husband. The guests tossed rice over the couple and offered their congratulations.

The reception commenced right after the sunset. The banquet was filled with joy and touches of laughter. The speeches were full of love and humour. The band went onto the stage after the dessert was served. The married couple wowed their guests with a medley of choreographed moves with songs like Dirty Dance, Thriller, The Time of My Life, etc. Cheers and whistles showered the newlyweds from the beginning until the end.

When the first dance was over, the guests poured onto the dance floor and danced the night away in the airy marquee. Jessica enjoyed herself immensely. She was taking in the bliss of the picture in front of her when she felt her hand being held by someone.

"Come dance with me, will you?" Luke appeared in front of her, looking deliciously handsome in his tailor-made designer suit. She'd been so occupied the whole day looking after all the details of the event as well as one of the grooms, she'd completely forgot about the guy she had just shown her bottom to two days ago.

"Uh, sure," Jessica recalled the scene at the waterfall and embarrassment washed over her. "Sorry for taking all my clothes off the other day." She wanted to explain to

Luke about the misunderstanding, but Luke couldn't hear her. Luke held his hand by his ear, signing to Jessica that he could hardly hear her over the loud music.

"I said I didn't mean to take all my clothes off in front of you the other day!" Jessica yelled. Just at that same moment, the band switched to soft, slow dance music to wind the evening down. People who were dancing around them paused and looked at Jessica. Everyone could hear what Jessica had just said. She wanted to find a hole and hide.

"Come with me." Luke offered his hand to Jessica and asked her to run away with him. Jessica put her hand into his, trusting the same man who put her into such a situation to come to her rescue. They walked and then ran far away from the reception.

They ran and ran until they were both out of breath. They heard waves crashing ashore and realised they'd arrived at the beach. Jessica reluctantly slid her hand off Luke's to take her heels off. They walked along the shore, and Jessica took the chance to explain herself to Luke.

"There… sorry for my ignorance and stripping at the waterfall." Jessica's confession was greeted by roars of laughter.

"Now, I am the one who is embarrassed. I totally took it as an invitation. I was so hurt that the stripping off was the end of it." Luke half-jokingly told Jessica how disappointed he was for the lack of action afterwards. "Shall we start fresh, now that we have established clearly regarding our sexual orientation?" Luke raised his fingers while placing the other hand on his heart. "I here solemnly declare I, Luke Hunter, like girls. And, I like you…" Luke looked Jessica straight into her eyes, which immediately turned her knees into jelly. He then gently held her face and gave her the softest kiss she had ever had.

Jessica spent the rest of her stay with Luke, but out of respect for Jessica, Luke did not try to sleep with her. He said he would like to ask her out on a date when they were back to Europe. He would take the Eurostar from Paris and spend the weekend in London with her. Jessica was in total bliss and said 'yes' to Luke.

***

"Hello, what's the occasion that deserves top-level effort from our Miss Ma?" Aisha, Jessica's flatmate, interrogated her when she saw her dressing up for her date with Luke. Aisha had been sharing her apartment with Jessica ever since Jessica moved to London. Parents on both sides welcomed the arrangement, with Jessica's parents trusting her daughter to live with a girl from a decent Indian family, and Aisha's parents felt comfortable for their daughter to live with a conservative Chinese flatmate.

"No one, just a friend who's come visit from Paris." Jessica casually dismissed her flatmate, only to be betrayed by her blush when she thought of Luke.

"Your face is burning! Come on, spill!" Aisha traded for the whole story out of Jessica by offering to take out the rubbish for the rest of the month.

"Oh, I envy you. Not only you have a sexy man coming all the way to see you, but your family has also progressed much since we've known each other. My parents are still very resistant to BMW," Aisha sighed.

"BMW? Are you thinking of getting a car?"

"Not that BMW. Black, Muslim or white is still a 'no, no' to most Indian families." Even though Aisha's parents had been living in the UK for the past three decades, they remained very traditional Indians. They still believed in arranged marriages with boys from families matching their hierarchy.

Indeed, Jessica had never thought of the possible issue it would raise if anything serious would come out of her dates with Luke. Yet, judging from her parents attending Jay's wedding, Jessica allowed herself to feel hopeful.

CHAPTER FIFTEEN

The company stamp weighed tonnes in Joanne's hand. She lifted it up with much difficulty, then pressed it hard down onto the sales and purchase agreements one after another on the desk in front of her. In the past five years, her father had gradually transferred most assets under the family company holdings, in which he and Joanne were directors. As her father's construction company had won tenders of government projects to develop the New Territories, he struggled to comprehend all the complex commercial and legal documents that were sent his way for approval and signatures. In the end, he decided to authorise Joanne as the sole signature required for all transactions and business accords. His second daughter was the most natural choice - as his eldest daughter Jacqueline had to maintain a role out of the family core business to act as their counsel. Joanne was known as the spinster in the family, and both Helen and Jaguar expected and accepted that Joanne would probably never get married and stay home forever.

In the past month, Joanne had consolidated the evaluation and tax filing situation of each of the families of whose lands Susan was interested in acquiring for her collaboration with the biggest developer in town to build eco-luxury villas - the first of its kind in the city - right at home in Ma's village. Once she had passed on the sensitive and supposedly confidential information with Susan, who then had their accountants drumming up respective orders, Joanne was only needed to fulfil her final promise; to drop the final axe that would alter the Ma's landscape in the area forever.

'Ma' means horse in Chinese. It is a symbol of elegance, regality, and strength for the local people. Looking at Ma's territory on a map, one would be astonished by how the lands formed into a shape that resembled a galloping horse. There were some small pieces of Ma's land scattered nearby, that looked almost like the dust kicked up by the stallion. So far, the lands or properties sold to outsiders concentrated on those outside the heart of the village. There were still many farmlands available for the male descendants of the Ma clan to claim and build houses on when they came of age.

However, the lands that Susan and her developer counterpart had their eyes on, together with the government lands, as well as the properties that Joanne had just sold to Susan, were about to cut the handsome animal in half. There was only one direction the future houses could be built, which was on the other side of the hill - a trough of a valley which was currently used as a junkyard by the villagers - while the side of the village that would eventually be sold off was a prime area that faced a stunning ocean.

For generations, Ma's lands had been blessed with sunshine, fertile soil, and pristine air. Striking trees took root along the village paths, and fragrant flowers bloomed in the villagers' garden. Day and night the village was filled with the harmonic orchestra of birds and insects. Outsiders were in awe of the unusual colours and patterns of the butterflies in the area. Besides being blessed by nature, the infrastructure was impeccable. A private road leads into that part of the village while still only being minutes away from the highway leading to the city. The surrounding area was an abundance of lushness.

The Government saw it as a perfect sample to assign it the city's first-ever eco-zone. The administration wished to relieve the population density in the city and encourage citizens to relocate outside the city in the rural land. The most effective way was, to begin with, exceptional and luxurious houses which would draw the public's attention, increase the property value in an otherwise less desirable area, and demonstrate the high quality of lifestyle the residents could enjoy by living there. Facilities and self-sustainable renewable energy infrastructure would be built throughout the complex, and the developer had the mission to integrate these structures as part of the living areas. The project would create a blueprint and set up a fine example for the Legco, the city's law-making body, to grant more budget and approved proposals to develop the rural lands in the New Territories to answer the ever-increasing demand of housing for the general population.

To everyone outside Ma's village, it was an exciting and innovative initiative which was going to bring enormous benefit to the general public as a whole as well as setting the city up as a leader in the region for sustainable housing and living. Sadly, for Joanne's family and her people, it was going to destroy the feature of their terrain and the legacy left by their ancestors forever.

Night after night, demons caught up with Joanne to debate whether she should or could do, what's been asked of her by Susan. She had never betrayed anyone, least of all her parents - whom she loved and hated at the same time. However, these days, the latter seemed to dominate her heart most of the time. She reminded herself that she was once a shy, but a joyful and innocent girl who was full of sweet dreams and hope for the future. She had had a wonderful and carefree childhood growing up in the village. Joanne and her siblings, along with their cousins and other children in the village were allowed to run wild on the hill, along the river, on the beach, in and out each other's garden and house. Everyone knew and looked out for each other. The sense of security and community was tight, which provided the cocoon for children to explore as much and as far as their curiosity would lead them. Those were some of the happiest days in Joanne's life, second only to the intimate moments spent with Christian.

Yet, those freedoms would be successively replaced by expected conducts, and protection would then be felt more like unwanted watches as one entered young adulthood. What used to be seen as carefree would be regarded as being frivolous. Joanne was taught to know her obligations and where her 'place' was. She was no longer her own person; each and every bit of her behaviour would reflect on both her family as well as on the village. A family's reputation seemed to rely heavily on the female members, instead of the male, even though most fortune and privileges flew to the other direction of the gender line.

Around the same time as her forced abortion, her cousin Stanley had knocked up his classmate at his high school. Not only was Stanley not punished for his 'crime,' as was the case for Joanne, his parents supported the young couple through the gunshot wedding and celebrated the arrival of their baby boy, who would continue the bloodline of the family, as well as adding fortune to the already amounted wealth of the lineage. On the contrary, what Joanne's parents did to her destroyed all that was good and left her the bereft woman she was today. These days the village brought her only sorrow and remained as a constant reminder of the tragedy that out-dated, ancestral traditions and beliefs would bring.

As to boost to her determination, she contacted the house owner in Portugal whose Airbnb property she wanted to rent for the first few months she wanted to stay at while she took care of Christian's ashes, and find out whether she liked the place enough to commit for a more long term investment. She had no immediate plans to have kids yet, but she believed it caused no harm to identify a fertility clinic in Spain to freeze her eggs already. She wondered if she would ever have the courage to let another man into her heart. She told herself to keep an open mind as everything was possible once she left the suffocating and demurring environment that she had grown up in. Joanne also checked the air tickets to Lisbon. The flights did not operate daily so she made a mental note that she must coordinate with Susan to make sure she could fly out right away or before anyone in the family could learn about her selling out of the clan.

***

"Wow, you have some incredible talents, Jessica."

Jessica had invited Luke to the annual summer exhibition along with the flower show at the botanical garden managed by her employer and sponsor. Luke was impressed by Jessica's artworks, whose works were the highlight of the show.

"Thank you, I have the racial advantage to dominate the exhibition due to the number of visitors from Asia during the summer holiday. My boss displayed my works intending to attract more donors from the 'crazy rich Asians.'" Jessica had been worried that Luke would find the exhibition boring, but to her surprise, Luke showed genuine interest in what she did and even engaged in some interesting conversations with her colleagues. One of her colleagues teased her by mouthing the word 'keeper' to her when Luke was not looking.

"And why is there a spider in all your signatures? A fan of Spiderman?" Luke raised one of his eyebrows. Other than being a computer geek, he loved comic books. Spiderman and Batman were his all-time favourite superheroes.

"Now you are pulling my leg. When I first started drawing plants, I was often scared to hell by the spiders. We had lots and lots of them where I come from. I was quite discouraged, and I once thought of giving up because I was too afraid of spiders. Then one day, when a spider stopped me from advancing, I saw this amazing flora. I did a portrait on it which had become one of my best works ever. Since then, my whole mindset shifted, and I gradually got used to the sight of them. I always include a spider in my signature to remind myself not to forget to pause every now and then to notice the beauties around me."

"That's very profound, I love it. And I apologise for being a dick. You do have quite a distinctive style compared to other works here, am I wrong? Excuse me if I am, obviously, I know nothing about art, I am just a computer geek, after all."

"You have a pair of pretty good eyes for a computer geek. I have not received any proper art training. I acquired most of my art skills from my grandpa, who loved gardening and painting in Picasso style. He taught me everything about trees and flowers. I did a botanical art course to learn about the biology of the plant and technical skills to draw them. I think over time, I've developed a style of my own that's a hybrid of my grandfather's and my training. My grandfather stressed the importance of imprinting a soul into every art piece I created - that's what draws attention and touches the viewer's heart. You can only communicate with your audience if, and only if, you can trigger an emotion in them. Every piece of my works here is actually the results of many visits to record different stages of the life of the same plant. I go back numerous times to their habitats to capture their essence over time. Each time they tell you more of their life stories. As long as you open your heart and keep an open mind to listen, they will hold no secret from you." Jessica's eyes sparkled when she talked about her works.

"That's deep, probably too deep for a computer geek like me."

Jessica gave Luke's bicep a playful punch for mocking her.

They had an idyllic afternoon at the botanical garden. There were streams of visitors made up of flowers lovers and tourists, from all over the world. Jessica knew the place inside out, and she found corners and hidden courtyards to steal private moments with Luke. Jessica felt like a teenage girl all over again.

Since then, Jessica and Luke took turns to commute between London and Paris to be with each other. They spent a wonderful Christmas in London with Jessica's friends as well as Luke's family in Bristol. It was Jessica's first time to visit the English city in the southwest. She loved the colourful industrial buildings by the wharf, the energetic and creative ambience, the multi-cultural and racial mix there due to historical reasons, and its open-minded crowd. For the first time since she left her childhood village home and settled in a foreign country, she felt right at home.

Chapter Sixteen

Plum blossoms and pots of Chinese mandarins lined up on both sides of the road leading to Ma village. Looking up, flags of Ma's family crest were flying nearly as high as the lamp posts. Firecracker explosions could be heard in the distance every now and then. Red banners of auspicious messages were pasted around the door of every village house. The atmosphere was festive and cheerful; one did not need to understand the culture to feel the celebratory pulse once entering the village.

"Are you ready?" Jessica turned to look at Luke and let go of his hand. It was a very bold act of her to bring her boyfriend back for Chinese New Year - but it would be too long for Jessica to go for without seeing Luke. There's no escape for her not to be home for the most important occasion in the Chinese culture. Besides, she had to draw portraits of flowers that blossomed during the spring festival for her next show. It was also time for her to have a follow-up meeting with the Chinese Medicine team of the local university she was collaborating with. She would have to stay for a month to accomplish it all. On the other hand, Luke was curious about the city and all the village stories Jessica had told him.

In the end, Jessica decided to invite Luke to come to join her, and her good friend Wolfgang, who's a computer game designer from the US volunteered to host Luke during his stay - so she did not have to confront with her family about bringing a non-Chinese boyfriend home.

"Yes, I am excited already. Look at all these 'Game of Thrones' setups." Admiring the theatrical picture in front of him, Luke thought he was in a movie. Wolfgang roared with laughter, and Jessica rolled her eyes. She hoped Luke would be able to find touches of humour in his experience all the way until the end. She'd already given Luke a heads up that she would not be able to spend much time with him, especially during the week of Chinese New Year. She emphasised no holding hands nor PDA's, or even exchange of looks outside of Wolfgang's house. He's on his own or with Wolfgang until she's free of her family obligations, then she could take him out to explore the city.

***

Jessica had not been back since Patrick Lee's funeral. She had not seen her family for several months; since Jay's wedding at Napa Valley, either. Yet, not much had changed in the village. The festive decorations remained the same as how it was when she grew up. The only change and growth she could count on was the papaya tree in the back garden of her childhood home. The main chunk had grown at least a foot taller, and there was another baby papaya tree branching out on the lowest tier. She wondered what else was new.

She had not had much communication with anyone either because of year-end and her travelling with Luke. Chinese New Year this year was particularly early, as it rarely fell in January. Because of its vicinity to Christmas, Jessica thought it would be fine to catch up with everyone when she was home for the red packet season. Jessica arrived on the day before the first day of the Chinese New Year on purpose. She had learnt her lesson that if she arrived two days prior, she would have to enslave herself helping her mother to do the spring cleaning, amid jet-lag and fatigue after a long-haul flight in economy class.

Moreover, everyone would be in a joyful mood and busy preparing to welcome the new year on the lunar calendar. Her parents would pay her little attention. She'd be free to roam around and do her own things.

First thing Jessica wanted to do was to pay a visit to her friend Mabel. She had not heard from her since their last phone conversation after Mabel's unfortunate miscarriage. Janice reported back to her that she did go check on her but Mabel refused any social call. After that, time just slipped away with Jay's wedding and her hanging out with Luke every single free moment she got. As she was drumming up excuses for her not being there enough for her childhood friend, she was pleasantly surprised when a pregnant, cheerful Mabel opened the door and welcomed her into her house. Her three girls rushed to Jessica after spotting her carrying gifts and had no doubt they were for them.

"Congratulations! What great news!" Jessica was speechless while at the same time relieved to see her friend who was devastated six months ago to be smiling again.

"Kenneth and I had our second honeymoon in Thailand, while I had another IVF. We could choose the gender of the embryo to put in me. There is one healthy, chubby baby boy baking inside now," Mabel rubbed her tummy and announced proudly.

"Oh, I am so happy for you. When are you due?" Jessica gave Mabel a bear hug, happy for her friend as well as for herself for getting off an otherwise difficult visit.

"End of June, it's going to be torture towards the end of the pregnancy in the summer heat. But I am going to endure it for this little prince. My boy and your nephew are going to be buddies, isn't it great?" Mabel grinned.

"Jacqueline is going to have a girl." Jessica's eldest sister had announced her pregnancy at Jay's wedding, and she's about to pop any day from now."

"I am talking about Janice. You didn't know? She's pregnant with her second one, a baby boy, too! I can't wait for our little ones to have playdates together."

Jessica was in shock. She had no idea that Janice, her closest sister, was pregnant. They had a fallout a few months back when she found out Janice had an abortion after finding out the sex of the baby. She didn't mean to tell anyone, it just slipped out her mouth when they were talking about Mabel. Janice thought Mabel was weak and did not have what it took to become a power wife that could survive in the village culture. The two sisters had an intense debate over the fate of a baby girl born in an indigenous family. Jessica believed that there was a world and a life outside the village. She gave herself as an example as well as their cousins such as Susan and Sarah. However, Janice disagreed. To her, it's better to be born with privileges than tempting fate, which she believed being born female was already losing half the battle - leaving aside the fact that giving birth to a girl would weaken her position, which was more important than ever, in the face of the power struggle between her and her mother-in-law, Barbara.

***

The Year of Monkey arrived as the first string of firecrackers went off at 7 o'clock in the morning. Luke had never seen anything like this in his entire life. The firecracker strip must be at least fifty meters long. He wondered who in the village had the guts and the strength to climb all the way up to the top of a lamp post to wind the firecracker vine over it. It took nearly fifteen minutes for the whole vine to burn off.

It was a jolly scene back home. Jacqueline was about to give birth to her first child. Jessica's eldest sister was over the moon to be pregnant after years of trying. Both Jacqueline and Simon were very excited to be welcoming their baby girl at any time, despite Helen already urging them to have a boy right after. Janice was pregnant with her second boy. Her face was glowing, and she had an air of superiority beaming off her. She seemed to have forgotten her row with Jessica and was warm as usual towards her little sister. Jessica sighed a huge relief.

Even Joe had softened up and seemed to have matured a bit in his behaviour, and Jessica was shocked to learn that he was going to become a father in less than four months. His latest girlfriend managed to get herself knocked up by the heir of the Ma family. She was only twenty-two, a very young age these days to have a baby. But since they found out she is going to have a boy, she has been welcomed to the family with open arms. Helen insisted that they were going to get married before her grandchild was born.

To Jessica's surprise, her second sister, Joanne, who was never a sociable person, was seen out and about. She took the initiative to come talk to Jessica and asked her about her work in London. Jay also brought Tony home, officially, and introduced him to everyone. It was their first Chinese New Year as a married couple. They prepared red packets for all the kids in the village. Everyone welcomed them, and no one refused their lucky money because they were gay! 'Money is money' as the kids could not wait to spend their money away at the kiosks on candies, crisps, chocolate, and little toys they could get from the vending machines.

Wolfgang brought Luke to the village dinner, which was held according to custom, on the second day of the New Year. More than a hundred of tables were set up, and 'Poon Choi' was served. 'Poon Choi' literally meant big bowl feast; it was a village tradition in Southern China in which courses of food was presented in layers within a big metal basin. Jessica told Luke the origin of it - that there was an emperor who fled to a village, and the villagers wanted to serve their best food available, but because of a lack of containers to serve the whole army, they piled the food up in an enticing manner, but all in a big wooden bowl. Luke was fascinated by the story, as well as the lion dance performance before the village dinner commenced. Wolfgang introduced Luke to Jessica's family, knowing that the hospitable leading family in the village would invite them to join their table. Jessica had purposely left the stool next to her empty and reserved it for Luke. So far, her scheme had gone perfectly. Everyone thought that Luke was Wolfgang's guest, and Luke was having a grand time in Ma's village.

***

Joanne took in the scene in front of her. It was going to be her last village dinner. She had lots of fond memories of such dinner parties when she was a little girl. She and her sibling chased after each other, waves of laughter, and the clinking of beer glasses to drink bottom-up from the adults filled the vast space on the village green field. For the last decade, it felt more like a forced appearance for her. This year was no different. She envied her siblings, who were about to welcome new members to the family, with much bitterness. Everyone in her immediate family knew what happened, although, over the years, no one had an ounce of sensitivity whenever they talked about pregnancies and babies. She looked forward to escaping to a place where there would be no more baby talks, and no comparison would be made among siblings and cousins; where she could truly be herself, and by herself.

Joanne mustered her enthusiasm and wished everyone Kung Hei Fat Choi, good fortune for the year to come so that people had the impression of her still going to be around after her departure later that night. She'd intentionally booked her flight out on the evening of the village dinner, knowing that most of the villagers would be drunk and things would be quiet and slow over the next couple of days. It would be days before anyone noticed she's gone. She is going to lock her room up, so it would buy her some time before her mother suspected something. When eventually her parents realise she's gone, they would find a letter on her desk, explaining and confessing everything. She's going to take the blame to keep the peace between her father and Uncle Jimmy, as well as Susan, at best. She will also leave most of her belongings in her room, and take only a few items of sentimental value as well as some important documents. For the past two weeks, she'd made several trips into town to do some shopping, and filled two suitcases up and left them with Susan, who had arranged a pick up for her to leave the village to catch her late-night flight bound for Europe.

CHAPTER SEVENTEEN

"What have you done, Susan?!" Jimmy stormed into Susan's office. Jimmy shouted at Susan and told her about how devastated Jaguar was after realising Joanne's disappearance and reading her farewell note. Joanne had confessed about selling a handful of the landmarks in the Ma village, which Susan had already known all the details. She had completed buying off the properties required from the villagers, with the help of Joanne's suggested offers after studying everyone's book. The acquisition had gone smoothly. The owners were more than pleased to sell one or two properties out of the many they owned at a higher than market value, just before the Chinese New Year. It was always a good omen to begin a new year with a bonus in the pocket.

"Jaguar said Joanne claimed she had been scheming with Kellock House to launch a big, eco-building project adjacent to Ma's village. She wanted to get even for what he and Helen did to her and her baby years ago, as well as making a big commission to set herself up in a country far away from here. She did not steal any money, but apparently, she sold the village office, the ancestral hall, the village temple and several other key buildings in the village. He asked me if we could help to undo what Joanne had done. You tell me." Jimmy scratched his head and still could not believe that he saw no sign nor have any clue on his daughter carrying out such revenge with Joanne. "What have you done behind my back, Susan? I know very well Joanne was not capable of orchestrating such deal and did not have the right contact at Kellock House without your involvement." Jimmy was enraged and demanded Susan to tell him everything.

"Daddy, it's a done deal. It's going to raise us up to the level as the big guys. And we can launch our IPO with this project." Susan then rolled up the map and 3D simulation landscaping to her father, expecting the reveal of her plan would calm him down and make him proud.

"Oh my god, nooo! We can't do that. Let's give Kellock back the money and ask them to find someone else. It's going to ruin the village as well as our family!" Jimmy was horrified by the destroying news his eldest daughter had just broken to him.

"I am afraid we can't. All the documents have been signed and submitted to the Government. We have received all the green lights to start planning and construction as soon as possible. Money has exchanged hands. If we withdraw now, not only are the penalties going to bankrupt us, there will be legal repercussions for all of us at the top management. Besides, Joanne wanted to do this - she's been paid fifty million to be the key facilitator." As Joanne had volunteered to take all the blame, Susan did not hesitate to take advantage of that, since she's now the one in the heat of the whole fall out.

"You are using Joanne's rage to get what you want. You used her! We cannot do that to our people. Those are our roots. Without the root, everything growing from it will die!" Jimmy's chest heaved up and down, and he found himself getting out of breath. It seemed both he and his brother had lost their control over their children.

"Daddy, don't you think it's unfair that Uncle Jaguar was born with everything while we had to earn everything here because you were born two minutes after him? 'If we cannot be born with privileges, we go create our own.' You taught us this, don't you remember?" The more they debated about it, the more Susan got worked up. She always thought that was the drive behind the company - her father and among her siblings - that they were born second, but they could work to the top with diligence and strong will.

"Jaguar and I love each other. And we love our village and people. Although it looks like my brother has everything, he always has my back. In fact, he has everybody's back. He never claims any credits and helps everyone in need quietly. He let everybody think that I built all this up from nothing. It's not entirely true. Of course, I worked hard. We all work very hard to get to where we are. Remember the few close calls we had in the past that we nearly lost everything? It's my brother, the secret investor, who loaned us the money; the money we have never returned, to sail through one crisis after another. Without him and the village, we could not have anything we have now. I beg you, we need to turn things around. Look at this," Jimmy pointed at the map with his shaking finger, "there will be no more horse in the Ma village. You have just sold its body off!"

***

Back in the village, the puzzle started to come together. Villagers began to report to the village office about the sale of their properties. It was a rule within the village that any sale of a village property from an indigenous villager to an outsider must be reported to the chief within thirty days of completion. Jacqueline had just given birth to her baby daughter two days ago, and she was summoned urgently back home to make sense of all the sudden transactions and sales of the most important village buildings by Joanne.

Jacqueline, exhausted from her labour while also being overwhelmed with joy from the arrival of her angel baby girl, Catherine, was torn between her obligation to her family, village, and that to her new-born baby. In the end, she had to carry little Kate around, and an inflated hoop to relieve pressure from the tear of her backside, to help her father to make sense of everything and find a solution to rescue the village.

Jacqueline's heart jumped when she saw all the transactions belonged to one buyer. She quickly investigated and found out it was a subsidiary of the most established real estate developer in town. She rang up her counterpart over there, and in no time Jacqueline learnt about the details of Susan's deal with them, as the lawyer of the firm thought she wanted to clarify the legal details of the agreement.

Pushing the pram down the corridor, Jacqueline marched into Susan's office. Susan thought it was déjà vu, as her father did the other day. She wondered whether the storm would ever die down.

"So you know?" Susan asked Jacqueline calmly.

"Yes, and so does everybody back home. Why? Why did you do that? I can understand Joanne's hatred, but why did you teach her to make such revenge that would destroy our village and break our family apart?" Jacqueline could not believe her cousin had the heart for such betrayal. She blamed herself for overlooking things as she was only working part-time towards the end of her pregnancy.

"It was only a matter of time that someone would do it. All the developers and the Government had been eyeing our lands for a very long time. Now we are part of the project, we CAN have a say and an influence to what the area would become. Have you seen the plan yet? It's going to a good thing for the area; it will bring the property prices up too, and we will all benefit." Susan tried to divert the attention to the overall good the project would do.

"There's no more WE when you decided to sell us out." Jacqueline turned and left Susan's office with a wailing newborn, leaving Susan to pondered on her last comment.

***

Everyone in the house reacted differently to the situation once learning the scale of devastation of Joanne's actions. Helen was heartbroken for her daughter's departure and blamed herself for manifesting such a deed, because of what she and her husband did to Joanne a decade ago. Jay was sad to see his sister gone, but secretly happy for her to be free of the suffocation she had been feeling from her family and the demons that had been following her around. Janice was amazed by what her introvert sister did and saluted her wherever Joanne was - she was proud of what she did; she now belonged to the Lee clan and did not feel too much of a loss. Jessica cared little about the loss of wealth nor land but she was hurt to see her family in agony and most of all, she felt guilty of being ignorant of the pain her second sister had been living in. No one had ever gauged the damage done to Joanne years ago when she was forced to end her pregnancy, hence did not give the healing she needed. Jessica mourned her departure and in her heart wished her all the happiness that she deserved.

Joe was the one whose reaction scared everyone. The usual do-not-give-a-damn and entitled Joe was furious by his sister's betrayal. It turned out Joe knew the family's assets like the back of his hands, and the whole family was astonished by him questioning his father on each property one by one, and how it was going to impact the fortune, he was born to inherit.

"That bitch! If I find her, I am going to strangle her with my bare hands!" Joe's ears were bright red after Jaguar revealed to everyone how all the prime lands in the village now belonged to the biggest land developer in the city as well as the Government. Not only that - but the implication also forever remodelled future land allocation when a male indigenous descendant claimed a piece of land to build his 'small house.'

***

"I am gutted to see my family divided like this, and of course, my sister's gone." Jessica was trying to seek all the comfort she could from Luke at times like this.

"I am not an expert in any of this, I love everything I see and everyone I've met here so far. But from what you're telling me, don't you think the whole village business and how male descendants inherit land was out of date?" Luke had learnt much about the history and politics of the village from both Jessica and Wolfgang. Wolfgang told Luke how he admired his courage to date an indigenous girl.

"You laugh about how this looks like 'Game of Thrones'? IT IS game of thrones," Wolfgang mocked Luke one day while explaining to Luke all the chemistry between locals and outsiders in the village; the Dos and Don'ts that he'd learnt throughout the years he'd been living among the indigenous people. "As long as you mind your own business and don't act in a way that would disturb the harmony of everything the village people believe in, you are welcome and will be left in peace here."

"Yes, it's unfair that only male descendants can inherit the land, and it's probably ridiculous these days when so many people are crammed into a tiny living space in the city, and everyone here lives in such a big house to justify such policy to continue. Please don't forget, though, all these lands belonged to our ancestor's generations and generations ago. It was out of goodwill that our people agreed to such a policy to help to ease the living demand from the general population. Our people had contributed much to each administration, and are continuing to do so. My father's company was an indispensable effort to develop this whole area in the New Territories and beyond. No one knows the land and how every inch of it reacted to different construction like us. We are more useful than the Royal Family to the British." Jessica was surprised to find how defensive she was to her culture and tradition that denied her right to any of the privileges because of her gender.

"Wow, wow, wow, calm down Khalessi. I totally get where you come from. So what do you think is going to happen?"

"I have no idea. I am only a botanical artist and a daughter of an indigenous villager. I don't know what I can do to help."

Chapter Eighteen

Jimmy pushed open the door to the village temple, which was already ajar. He was looking around for Jaguar and guessed he could find him here. Jaguar was kneeling down in front of the altar where the wooden boards of all their ancestors were erected. He repeated his apologies for not being able to protect the village he'd been commissioned with and prayed for their forgiveness. It broke Jimmy's heart to see his brother beating himself up like that. For the past week, he'd been working day and night with Sarah, Susan, and their team of lawyers and accountants to see if they could turn things around. Regrettably, as the Government was involved, no money nor power would be able to get them out of the deal. Jimmy knelt down next to Jaguar and explained to his ancestors that the faults were all his. He and Jaguar then debated with each other and fought for taking the bigger blame as if there was an actual panel of judges sitting in front of them.

"I blame myself for not being around enough, and not having shown enough to my children how much I love them, how much they mean to me." Jaguar eyes turned red when he thought how he wished he'd been a better father.

"No, the faults are all mine. It's my Susan who gave Joanne such an evil idea to betray us all. I shouldn't have given the girls so much power within the company. I am responsible for all and for Joanne's running away. I am so sorry, please forgive me."

"Don't ever say that, brother. You did right and great the way you brought up Susan and Sarah. That's what Helen and I should have done in the first place. Treasure our girls as much as we do our boys. Let them develop their interests and talents that they have been blessed with. Look at your girls, the first-ever CEO and COO ever produced in any villages in Hong Kong. Who'd dare to say you haven't done a damn good job raising them?" Jaguar hit his fist on the altar table as to challenge anyone who would think otherwise.

"And of course I forgive you. We love and forgive each other. That's what families do."

Jimmy fell into Jaguar's arms and cried. There was a deep bond between the twins even when both their hair was turning white. Together they grieved for the village's future.

***

On the other hand, Jacqueline gathered all the villagers who had sold their properties to the project at the village office. Strictly speaking, that building along with her own office no longer belonged to them. She had not spoken to Susan nor Uncle Jimmy ever since she'd confronted her cousin. Her professional self was telling her to go through all contracts and agreements before any action, while her emotional self-propelled her to do whatever she could and as soon as possible. She hardly had any sleep these days. She had to nurse little Kate on demand. She was lost about what she should do to help or save her family. She could not feel any joy from the fact that she'd finally become a mother after years of waiting and longing for a baby. She was confused with whether she had postpartum depression or the negative emotions were all due to the crisis she and the village were facing. In any case, she was going to convince all recent house sellers to voluntarily buy back the properties they sold. She was going to offer to them that her father would pay for all the taxes and processing charges so that they would not suffer any loss. She'd do the same for all the village building which deeds once belonged to her family's holding company.

"But I will never be able to sell my house at this price. My house is really in an isolated spot of the village; I don't think it'll make any difference if I buy it back or not," one villager questioned.

"The developer explained to us what they are going to do. I actually think it would be good for both Hong Kong and our village. The development will definitely increase the property value of this area," another villager reflected.

"Now if I think more about it, the only one who has anything to lose is your family!" Then everyone talked and said wanted to give an opinion.

Most of them were not in favour of what Jacqueline would like to ask from them, and she was soon attacked by a migraine and had to call the meeting off. She was relieved to run back home. At one point, she feared they were going to attack her and the little angel she was cradling in her arms.

The day after Jacqueline failed to rally other villagers to support the village chief and undo the transaction of the sale of their properties, both Jaguar's and Jimmy's children, except Susan, got together at Jaguar's house to try to find a solution to minimise the damage.

"Who refused to cooperate? I'll go and beat their sons up." Joe rolled up his sleeves and demanded to know which villagers refused to comply.

In fact, not one of them saw it such a grave situation that they had to part with their multimillion dollars. The properties that they sold were more on the outer edge of the village. They had sold houses before on more prominent lands. They only knew the alarm was caused by the fact that all their houses had been acquired by a big land developer. They did not know that together with the main village buildings at the front of the village that had been sold to the same buyer by Joanne, a boundary had been created that pushed the whole village back. Any future houses would have to be built on the back of the village, the rather undesirable side of land in every villager's eye.

"We can't really accuse them of any wrongdoing. We haven't told them what actually is going on. How can we? How can we tell them that their own people had betrayed them? We are supposed to look out for them, for the whole village, not selling them out." Jaguar covered his face with his hands. He could not imagine how he was going to face his people and tell them that from now on their sons' houses would have to be built on the other side of the village; on the junkyard instead of the sea-facing, fertile land that they believed was theirs to nurture their future generations.

Jay wanted to say something but stopped himself before any words could come out. He decided not to push his luck after his parents had accepted Tony into the family. In fact, he told himself that it would not be fair for him to say his piece as the future planning of the village had little impact on him. He was not going to inherit anything except his own 'small house,' which was already under construction after he and Tony approved the design, which was a wedding gift from his architect and interior designer cousin. Suddenly, a question dawned on him: if he and Tony decided to have a baby later, as many of their friends in California did through a surrogate, would their baby boy be entitled to a 'small house'? He'd never cared much about such privilege before, but if it's something his future children would be entitled to, he felt he was obliged to fight for them. Yet, he did not think it was time to raise such a question. He footnoted his idea and query so he could discuss with Tony later. For now, he was there to support his family, especially to give comfort to his mother, who had been a wreck ever since Joanne's disappearance.

"It was my idea to take Joanne to the clinic. I thought I was doing her a favour so she could have the future of a proper marriage later. I ruined her life. It's all my fault. It's karma." Helen was speaking in such a low voice, then everyone realised she was talking to herself. She repeated the same thing again and again, which was worrying. Jaguar gestured Jay to take his mother back into their bedroom.

"Susan had sent me all the legal documents, and I trawled all over them throughout the night. There was no loophole in any of the transactions or planning. There's no way we can undo the trade, nor we could challenge the Government to abort the planning. The public response is mostly positive, so we are completely on our own to fight this battle," Jacqueline explained. She was yawning and had dark circles below her eyes.

Sarah was there to act as a mediator. She promised her father that she would answer all her cousins' enquiries truthfully after Susan finally shared with her and her brother what was in the pipeline for the company. She was grateful for Sarah not having involved her nor Anthony. Her loyalty had long gone to the company they built from scratch. In fact, both her work as a COO and Anthony's as the leading architect would only begin once Susan had locked the project in for the company. Despite the fact that she did not want to see any of her families hurt in the process, she saw the move as a definite positive direction; that the village was progressing. It was inevitable for the Government to develop the countryside to answer the ever-growing housing demands in the city. The new development was innovative and had sustainability in its planning. Anthony was eager to start working on the design once he had his hand on the guidelines and specifications. He already had many ideas in his mind. It was an opportunity he had been waiting for years for. A project like this would differentiate him from other architects in the city. He could eventually build a name of his own, instead of being the son of a property tycoon. Unlike their father, their attachment to the village was merely a childhood memory and a place they returned to once a year to celebrate Chinese New Year.

Janice was there more to gather intel as the drama unfolded. She had a certain knowledge of how development like the current project worked. She knew very well that there was no way anyone could turn anything around. She paid a quiet visit to Susan the other day as soon as she'd learnt about what happened. She congratulated Susan for her accomplishment. Susan rewarded her diplomacy with a verbal promise of giving her priority ahead of all the other real estate agencies to sell the unprecedented eco-luxury villas.

Jessica anticipated today's meeting was going to yield a solution. She could not believe with all the bright minds of her siblings and cousins, nothing could be done to save the village's future. Although she personally was not going to benefit from any of the outcomes, she had the urge inside her to help her family. It frustrated and upset her to see how this development was going to break her family. She left everyone in the heat of discussion but lack of conclusion. She went to the one place she could find strength and comfort from.

***

"Grandpapa, have you heard about what happened?" Jessica found her grandfather painting a new canvas in his front yard.

Jackson wiped his paintbrushes and his fingers. He joined Jessica and sat down on the step next to her.

"You know dear, I never asked for any of this." Jackson drew a big circle in the air and tried to include as much of a village as he could. "Privileges also come with responsibilities, many of them indeed. Did I tell you that I opened a bottle of champagne to celebrate the day your father moved into the big house? We had our glory in the village, but all of this cannot keep going forever. There is bound to be someone jealous about what we can get for just being who we are. We are just buying our time. The sooner we learn to be content with what we already have, the better, and happier. It's time for your father to see your Uncle Jakey."

Jessica leaned her head onto her grandfather's shoulder, sincerely hoping that her uncle would have the power to heal the wound of her family.

Chapter Nineteen

The villagers gradually caught wind of the grave future that awaited the village. After the Chinese New Year, the Government had announced publicly its plan to rejuvenate the countryside and to launch an unprecedented, pioneer project of environmentally sustainable houses. The news was very much welcomed by society across the sectors. The luxurious development meant the value of properties in the countryside would appreciate, which encouraged citizens to buy and move out of the centre of the city, providing the much-needed relief to the ever-rising population. However, as soon as the villagers saw the outlined area of the development on the map printed in the newspaper, it caused an uproar in the village.

"My son is going to get married next year and will want to build a house. Where will he be able to do that?" one villager asked.

"I have three teenage boys, and I've been saving money for them to build their houses as soon as they are of age," another cut in.

"I am sure our chief already has a better plan for us. He must have a deal with the government and preserved some good pieces of land for our children and grandchildren," someone suggested.

Since there had been no meeting called, they ran to the village chief's house, and now there was a crowd gathered in his garden.

Jimmy was in the house with Jaguar, reading the same newspaper that caused such a reaction from the villagers. They had stayed up the whole night and discussed their options. By dawn, they'd made peace with the fact there was nothing they could do to reverse the outcome. They had decided they would hire the best architect and landscaper in the city to do whatever possible and needed to make the land on the other side of the village desirable. Jimmy would set aside twenty per cent of his company profit to set up a fund for that purpose and to compensate the villagers affected. If the villagers were still not satisfied, they were also willing to swap the prime lands where they had built houses. They also made the decision not to disclose any of the details and betrayals of both Joanne and Susan to preserve their daughter's reputation and dignity.

Jaguar shared their plan with the concerned villagers. Once he mentioned about Jimmy's company, IPO launch and profit-sharing, the villagers forgot all about the lands that had been sold or taken back by the Government, for now. Watching the villagers disperse and leave the courtyard one by one, Jaguar stood next to Jimmy, their arms over each other's shoulder, giving one another support and showing their fraternal unity that nothing could break.

When the city resumed its commercial activities after the Chinese New Year holiday, Kellock House sent representatives to the Ma village to take over the properties that were now owned by a management company who would oversee the whole project.

Still recovering from giving birth to Baby Kate, Jacqueline limped around to direct her secretaries to categorise and box up her more than a decade long law practices. She could always use the office at Uncle Jimmy's company as her permanent base. She and Simon had discussed the possibility to move out to the city to be within the zone of schools that they would like to send Baby Kate to one day. The irony of being born as a girl to an indigenous villager, even when a crisis struck, did not affect her much - at least from the materialistic point of view.

On the other hand, villagers were requested to go to the ancestral hall to remove their ancestors' wooden boards that had resided in the temple for generations. Jaguar promised he would rebuild another one, bigger and nicer, right away. Meanwhile, they would have to take shelter under a marquee that had been stood up overnight where the annual village party was held.

Jessica dove into her work and researches with the local university. She worked extra hard on this trip. She wanted to finish her work ahead of schedule so she could have days that she could focus entirely on showing Luke around. She cheekily brought Luke with her to the meetings with her academic counterparts, introducing Luke as her intern to help her take notes. Everyone was impressed by Luke and thought he looked more like Jessica's bodyguard. Luke bantered back telling them he worked part-time as a bouncer at various clubs in London.

In the last week of her stay before leaving, Jessica and Luke rose early one morning, in her own childhood home and Wolfgang's house respectively. Jessica was going to show Luke around the village as it was still was today. She knew that when she came home next, to the village she had known since she was a little girl, it would no longer be the same. They had to be out at the hours when everyone was still in bed.

"The picturesque scene and the colours of the first light will worth your while," Jessica promised Luke. "I am sorry you came at such a chaotic time. It's supposed to be mostly joyous moments this time of the year. What happened was unheard of, ever, in any village. I hope it hasn't scared you away. Has it?" Jessica wondered what Luke had to say witnessing all the drama happening in the village.

"Honestly? I think it's quite perfect timing for me to be here. It's better than watching Netflix." Luke pulled Jessica to him and gave her a big squeeze, allowing Jessica a perfect angle to give his chest a slight punch. They hadn't had many private moments together, and they missed being physically close to each other. They looked around, made sure the area was deserted, held hands, and walked closely side by side down the path.

"Look, this is Aquilaria Sinensis, the Incense Tree. We have quite a few of these in the village. It's a type of Feng Shui wood; therefore, it is highly valued by the villagers; otherwise, it would have been cut down a long time ago for making incense. It's highly fragrant and used commercially as agarwood. Come, can you smell it?" Jessica led Luke over to get close to the trunk. "Do you remember on some of my plant artworks I zoomed into the trunk. It's because every trunk has its unique pattern and the trunk is the first thing you see when you walk close to a tree. Take in the aroma and put your hand here to feel the texture. These are the senses you can only experience when you are in contact with nature."

"Don't ever say that you are JUST a botanical artist. You are nature's ambassador. You teach us, common people, to learn to admire the beauties around us. For this alone, I salute you." Luke gave Jessica a quick peck on her forehead.

Jessica and Luke let go of each other's hand when they heard some noise in the distance. It sounded like someone chopping something off. They looked at each other and walked to the direction of the sound to check out. Then they saw Jessica's father holding a tomahawk. He was chopping something near the root of a tree. Sensing someone approaching, Jaguar looked up and found Jessica, standing side by side with the black guy who was visiting one of his long-time white tenants, staring at him.

"Ahem, morning Dad, this is Luke, Wolfgang's friend from Europe. We ran into each other during our morning walk, jet-lag, very bad jet-lag. What are you doing here?" Jessica quickly found an excuse for her co-appearance with Luke and diverted the focus on whatever her father was doing to the tree.

"I am trying to uproot this tree and replant it on the other side of the village, where our village will be in future. These trees have been with us for hundreds of years. We cannot abandon them. If I cannot save our lands, at least I can save our trees."

"If you would like any help, I'll be happy to give you a hand," Luke offered.

Jessica immediately translated for her father, who was not used to Luke's heavy British accent.

"Tell this young man that I appreciate his offer. I have to do it all myself. Off you go, before all this mess soils your clothes."

***

Jessica then took Luke to the other side of the village to let him have a gauge of the shape the village is going to take with the unwelcome new development.

"You see why it is such a catastrophe for our village. Where we were standing with my father just now was most of our lands that have been sold to the developer, and are like, fertile, bathed in sunlight, and there's a constant flow of water streaming through from the peak of this mountain. Our ancestors believed it brings all the essence as well as blessings from up there down to everyone in the village. While here, it's like you are sitting in economy class on a plane and the person in front of you has his seat reclined. Sunlight rarely streams through even during the brightest hours of the day. All the sewage systems in the area, including those of our neighbouring villages, converge here. That's why there is a constant foul smell in the air. The lands that Joanne and other villagers have sold enclosed a big area of current government land but should have been allocated to the male descendants from our village when they come of age to build their own small houses. Now, these are the only plots left that belonged to our clan and eligible for future village expansion."

"Woah, it is indeed a difference between heaven and... junkyard," Luke said as he took in the scene in front of him. It was dark and grim, and he could see why everybody called it a junkyard. He could see broken pieces of furniture, a torn sofa, and burnt out appliances piled up everywhere, and it was just about a block away from where they were minutes ago - where butterflies and insects had their morning jam with some exotic birds. The whole village, even in the cold season, exploded in vivid colours of orange, shocking pink, and purple with the honeysuckle and bougainvillaea in full bloom.

"Do you think there's absolutely nothing that can be done to turn the verdict around?" Luke asked Jessica the same question she and her families had for a hundred time over the past week.

"No, my sisters, father, and even Joe had chewed on every single word on dozens of document to try to locate any clause or keywords that could touch on the borderline and allow us to appeal to the Government to reverse the transactions. Now, we should really start clearing this junk and blast part of this hill to let in more sunlight, unless there's a miracle, an act of God or nature…" Jessica stopped, and suddenly, an idea came to her. "The tree… the tree! Oh, I need to go stop Daddy." Jessica gave Luke a big and long kiss. "I love you. Go back to Wolfgang's house and wait for me there; I'll tell you everything later. Now I must go and speak with Daddy first."

Jessica ran back to where she found Jaguar.

"STOP! Daddy stop!"

Jaguar turned around and saw Jessica waving frantically while running towards him.

"Yes, I may need some muscles here, I could hardly dig the roots out, they are really deep into the ground." Jaguar was sweating profusely. The tree had not budged even an inch, no matter how Jaguar dropped his axe down on them.

"Daddy," Jessica paused and recovered from being out of breath, "Daddy, you need to stop, stop cutting the tree. Stop cutting any tree, NOW."

Chapter Twenty

"Daddy, I need you to stop cutting this tree, in fact, any tree in the village. Now!" Jessica repeated to her father while catching her breath.

"Well, I can't, even if I want to. This damn tree just won't give." Jaguar wiped the beads of sweat off his forehead and above his lips. "Why are you running out of breath? Is everything alright?" Jaguar was puzzled by his daughter's reaction. *The English air had made his daughter weird, just like it did to his father,* he thought to himself.

"It's not a damn tree, it may be THE tree who will save the village. I need to run now and ask grandpa something. I'll explain later. Just don't touch the tree." Jessica then picked up her pace again and ran to her grandparents' house.

***

"Grandpapa, I need you to come with me to verify a tree; I need you to tell me it is what I think it is." Jessica caught her grandfather, circling his arms and hips in the garden. It's the exercise routine Jackson did first thing every morning as soon as he got out of bed.

"You should know by now every single tree and plant in the village, Jessica," Jackson dismissed Jessica casually and continued his hip movements. He was a man of habits, and even with his favourite grandchild, he did not want his routine disrupted.

"Grandpapa, I might have found a way to save our village and family. I need you to come with me, now, to help me identify a tree and more if needed," Jessica pleaded with her grandfather.

Jackson then reluctantly followed Jessica out and briskly walked to where his son was. Jaguar had stopped, and he was now smoking a cigarette to cool himself down from the work.

"Grandpapa, what's this tree?" Jessica pointed at the one that her father wanted to uproot merely an hour ago.

"This is Tutcheria, you should be able to identify easily it from its flowers. Don't you remember what grandpapa taught you when you were little? It resembled 'a boiled egg cut into half.'" Jessica recited the last sentence together with her grandfather. Jackson was like a walking encyclopaedia when it came to flora and trees, and he taught Jessica everything he knew as she grew up. However, Jessica possessed some knowledge that would go even beyond her grandpapa, and she could hardly suppress her excitement.

Jaguar watched the exchange between his father and his youngest daughter. He could hardly catch a word that they said. He hated it when they spoke to each other in English.

"I love you, grandpapa." Jessica did a victory dance and gave her grandfather a big hug followed by a kiss on his face. Then she turned to her father and said, in Chinese, "Dad, I may have found a solution to save our lands."

***

Common Tutcheria, scientifically known as *Pyrenaria spectabilis* was a rare local species; its flowers were conspicuous, around four to seven centimetres in diameter, with nine to eleven rounded and overlapping sepals, and five to six showy white petals. The species was legally protected under the Forestry Regulations of the Hong Kong Government's Forests and Countryside Ordinance.*

Jessica had come to learn more about the different ordinances which protect species of florae and trees in Hong Kong from her collaboration with the local university. One of the missions of the Chinese Medicine Department was to identify endangered species and report them to the authority to preserve trees and plants that were of Chinese medicinal values and might face destruction or extinction in certain areas. They catalogued each of the herbs, shrubs, and trees, and kept them in a public archive such that their students, as well as nature lovers, could have easy access and play a role in their preservation.

For the practitioners, the Chinese medicine collected in the wild was far more effective and precious than those grown on the farm as the herbs would be more potent having survived adverse weather and climate through different seasons, storms and typhoons in its natural habitat.

The Government was keen on developing the city into a Chinese medicine hub in the region. Therefore, it was an important task for the academic department to carry out. Part of the collaboration with the Botanical Society was to have Jessica present the species concerned in a botanical aesthetic way to raise awareness among the public. She had been sent a full list of the concerned species with corresponding pictures so she could choose those that were of aesthetic values and turn into botanical art pieces. The plan was to create enough pieces to hold an exhibition. The show would then go on a world tour as a promotion of both Chinese medicine, and for the Botanical Society of London.

*Source: 'Portraits of Trees of Hong Kong and Southern China' by Sally Bunker, Richard MK Saunders and Chun-Chiu Pang

Once Jessica was certain of her findings as well as the evidence to support her case, she rang Jacqueline right away and told her everything. Jacqueline rushed back to the village and went through all the related documents Jessica had saved on her laptop. She then cross-checked the ordinances and their implications from her own resources. She even rang a few of her classmates at law school to seek their advice on similar cases. She broke into a big smile when she finished.

"Who would have thought? Who would have thought our baby sister would be the one who's going to save the day!" Jacqueline laughed and patted Jessica on the back.

That same afternoon, she filed a motion and submitted it to the court. Jessica and Jackson had identified three Common Tutcheria in the area that had been sold to the new development. According to the ordinance, the Government had an obligation to do whatever it could within its power to protect the concerned species as well as its habitat. Jacqueline knew very well that it did not matter if they would win the case in the end - the delay would be an incentive enough for the developer to give up the controversial part of the land, in order to proceed with the construction as per their schedule.

The village held its breath after Jacqueline's action. The following week, Susan received a call from Kellock House that they had to revise the location of their development, as one of the Government regulations had raised a red flag which might affect their progress later on. The newly assigned area was still close to the Ma village, but the majority of its area had shifted away from the village, as opposed to what was originally planned.

In the end, more than half of the Ma's land had been left out of the development. Susan informed her business partner that the villagers were willing to buy back the houses as well as farmlands which Kellock House had acquired from them at the same purchase prices, which was welcomed by the developer as the latest development would leave them the owner of an isolated area away from the main development. They were happy to get rid of them without suffering any loss. Jimmy had offered a fifteen per cent profit to those affect villagers for them to reverse the transaction they just did a month ago. His company was still steering towards launching its IPO. It was a win-win for all and a very happy ending to the crisis.

***

Jessica had never in her wildest dreams imagined such a day would come - that she would become the heroine to rescue her family out of a crisis. Her father and Uncle Jimmy thanked her profoundly. They were grateful for her action, and at the same time, impressed by their daughter and niece, who was merely a botanical artist. They decided to offer her one of the properties in the village as an expression of their gratitude. At first, Jessica refused to take it, thinking she actually did not do much to earn it but was immediately interjected by Janice.

"Take it, sis. You did 'earn' it. Have you realised how much money you have just given back to the village? Millions or even a billion! A village house these days is worth an average of twenty million dollars. The lands you have just saved were enough to build another dozen houses! Without the lands, those 'Dings' are worthless! If you don't want the house, I can sell it or let it out for you, and you can pocket the cash, but in any case, take it!"

Apparently, Luke agreed with what Janice said too. "If you feel bad about accepting such an expensive gift, do something good with it. I think you will make your family and everyone feel better if you accept it. I am so proud of you. You flew in and saved the day when everyone was about to surrender and admit defeat."

"I am not really sure if I have done the right thing. I actually liked the idea of having some eco-friendly houses to be built in the countryside. Hong Kong needs a more sustainable lifestyle. I hope the rescue of my family's lands does not mean the end of that project. The Ma's lands are definite, so it will come a day when it does not matter anymore whether you are born a boy or a girl, as the 'Ding' right does not give you the right to build a house if you have no land left. But I bet it is going to take generations before our people get to the level of that in the city when it comes to gender equality. For now, the birth of a baby boy means carrying on the bloodline and another house added to the family's bank that can be cashed in, in another eighteen years."

"Well, lucky we aren't going to have such a problem with our kids," Luke commented, and Jessica looked at him with an open mouth. Luke pulled her close and gave her the longest kiss they had ever shared. Things were going well between them.

Much had happened during the month they'd spent in the village, but it had only brought them closer to each other. Luke had a better grasp of Jessica's childhood and family background. He liked what he saw so far. Before his visit to Hong Kong, he admired Jessica for her talent in creating beautiful artworks on plants and trees. Now his admiration for her was from how she got to where and who she was from going beyond the limitation as well as imagination the village would otherwise have confined and defined her by. He had no doubt for her loyalty for she had displayed such loyalty to what she believed in, to her family, as well as to her own passion. Luke was almost certain by now that Jessica was the one for him.

***

The news had gradually spread across the village. For the remainder of Jessica's stay, no day passed without a villager bringing over some gifts to her door. There were red packets, eggs, roosters, pieces of jewellery, and even cars among the offerings. Some mothers also brought their daughters over and asked Jessica to teach them art. Except for the red packets, Jessica passed everything else over to her mother. She made a list of art institutions that Helen could pass onto other mums if they would like to enrol their children in. Although she had no interest in teaching yet, she thought it was a nice development for the villagers to appreciate both art and nature more. To Jessica, the biggest bonus of her trip was to be able to show Luke around, both in the city and the village where she'd grown up. She had long detached herself from the dogma of the place where she came from. She cherished the village where her core values were formed, families, traditions, integrity, gratitude, and unity. The village was an important and indispensable anchor of her life. However, she believed she needed to sail far away from it, to find her life purpose as well as to serve and be faithful to herself, and herself only.

Chapter Twenty-One

Joanne put her heavy shopping bag down onto the floor. There was a letter in her mailbox. She had not yet received any mail at her new address. No one knew where she was except Susan, although they communicated mainly via emails. She wondered if the mail was for the last occupant of her bungalow.

She'd found a charming, two-bedroom one storey house, in a small coastal town in Portugal. Her landlady was a widow and was open to selling as she would like to join her children in the city. Joanne told her she would make her an offer if she liked the place. For now, however, she was happy renting the lovely property sitting on a gentle cliff, looking out to the ocean.

Every morning she was greeted by the warm sun and sea breeze as soon as she opened her bedroom windows. She would do some yoga exercises as she was determined to get her body in shape for her fertility treatments when she was ready. After a shower, she would get dressed and walk down to the centre of the village. There was a community café where both residents and tourists liked to hang out in the morning, to enjoy their breakfast and pleasantries.

Within a short time, her days fell into a blissful routine. She would spend her days reading or exploring the country, where she allowed herself to make all day or short visits to neighbouring towns. She loved immersing herself into the beauties of foreign places, where she could ponder upon her past and begin her healing.

She turned the letter around and was surprised to find Hong Kong stamps glued onto the envelope. Her heartbeat picked up. The return address was the one she ran away from in the middle of the night about eight months ago. She tore open the letter right away; she needed to know if she should start packing and move.

The letter was from her parents - she recognised her father's handwriting. Susan had already told her about the chaos after things broke loose and how Jessica saved the day with her knowledge of trees in the village. To her relief, however, her father did not mention anything about her betrayal. Instead, Jaguar begged for her forgiveness for what he and Helen did to her fifteen years ago. He wrote they understood why she wanted to get away. He hoped she could find peace and happiness in her new home. They would be waiting for her news every day at home, and maybe one day, her return with open arms.

Joanne's hands shook, and she read the letter all over again. She had never thought the day would come when her parents would admit any wrongdoing for her abortion and the subsequent infertile outcome. She did not know whether she would ever have the heart to forgive them, but if her parents could come to admitting wrong and ask for her forgiveness... *maybe there's hope*, she thought, smiled, and moved on to sort out her groceries.

***

Jessica took a long last drag on her cigarette, picked up her weekend bag and walked into the house: her house. She'd flown all the way back for the inauguration of her house. It was once an ordinary village house that had been gifted to her for what she did to rescue more than at least half of the lands in the prime area of the Ma village.

After some serious considerations, Jessica decided to turn it into a multifunctional building. The ground floor had become an exhibition hall as well as a space for art classes and art jamming parties. She let the first floor to an NGO whose mission was to lobby and execute plans for the eco-friendly and sustainable living and development in the villages. She only charged the organisation a symbolic $1 annual rent, such that they could pour all their funding into resources in their practical programmes. The top floor and the garden rooftop was used as a retreat for both local and overseas artists. The accommodation was very affordable, and the guests were only charged a minimum to cover the utility bills as well as paying the cleaning staff of the house. The guests had to be able to produce at least two references from their fellow artists. Despite the attached condition, the rooms were fully booked all year round.

Thanks to her cousin Anthony, who had recently won some architect award for his design on an upcoming project, Jessica's house was cleverly designed to serve the different purposes of the building. Uncle Jimmy had footed the bill of the renovation and decoration. The villagers had volunteered their labour to speed up the completion. They were the ones who turned the overgrown bushes beside the house into a magical garden based on her grandfather's idea and vision. Jackson combined his extensive knowledge of plants with his artistic touch to turn the outdoor space of his granddaughter's new nest into a sensational garden that reminded him of those lovely rose gardens in England.

All the villagers and invited guests had arrived. Jessica got there just in time to cut the ribbon, not only for the opening of the house but also for the vernissage of her grandpapa's very first solo art exhibition. Jackson had painted hundreds of paintings in the last few decades. He chose thirty pieces with the theme of the village life, village gardens, as well as village children. It was the very first time any artists portrayed any village in Hong Kong in a Picasso style. The exhibition drew the attention of quite a number of art media, both locally and internationally. The sudden fame had made Jackson a celebrity overnight. He had been interviewed by magazines across the globe. Rich people knocked on his door to commission him on art pieces. It was a happy time for Jackson - not for the money but for the new purpose in his life.

Back at her parents' house, Joe and his wife had become the main masters of the house. Helen and Jaguar were still sleeping in their ensuite, but a spacious masters quarter had been built for Joe and his young family, by combining the six bedrooms with those of all his sibling's childhood bedrooms. Due to the reduction of prime lands to build new houses in the village, it was agreed that his parents would only have to move out to the house currently belonging to Rose and Jackson when they were no longer around. Joe was not entirely happy about the arrangement. He believed he was the one who'd had the most to lose in the whole episode caused by his sister's betrayal. However, no one would deny that Joe had matured after the arrival of his first son. He'd even started to learn his father's trade despite having never taken on any full-time job since he'd left school. His wife had convinced him the financial potential in the construction business after the announcement of 'One Belt, One Road' scheme introduced recently by the Chinese Communist Party.

Jessica stayed in her own house now in one of the artist's rooms. But everyone was expected to go back to their parents' house or Joe's house for family dinners. These days, the family dinners had become more lively because of the new young members. George was already a chatterbox and starting to walk. He adored his cousin Kate who loved crawling after him and found everything he did amusing. Janice had just given birth to another baby boy, Gregory, several months ago, and at dinner, she proudly announced she was eleven weeks pregnant with twin boys. It was an accident but a very welcome surprise. She was glowing with confidence and carried an air of superiority. She shared with Jessica that she was officially the first lady in the Lee village. Her mother-in-law Barbara wasn't doing very well these days. Her health had taken a blow by her recent defeat in court cases with her late husband's mistresses. A big chunk of her inheritance had been ruled to them by the court. Janice was going to be the mother of four male descendants in the biggest family of the biggest village in Hong Kong. Janice's flourishing real estate business due to the latest luxurious development also earned her much respect from her husband. She absolutely felt the world was her oyster.

Tony had settled well in the village. Everyone loved him, especially Grandma Rose. No one dared to make fun of him or call him names as everybody both respected and feared the 'Grandma with Thorns.' He and Jay were waiting for the grant of land to be approved for them to start building their house. Meanwhile, the couple had been flying back and forth between Hong Kong and California to meet with potential surrogates that could help them start a family. They initially wanted both of their sperms to be thrown into the same pool to fertilise the donor eggs so that they would have no idea whose sperm had resulted in their babies. In the end, however, Jacqueline talked them out of it, convincing them they should take turns - as if it was a boy, Jay should try to see if his son could be entitled to the 'Ding' right. Jay had never thought much of the possibility, but he decided that if there's a chance, he will fight for his child for what he's entitled to; his male descendant should not be any less than the other baby boys in the village just because both his parents were men. Jacqueline vowed to take his case to the highest court if needed to make sure her baby brother would not be discriminated against, solely because of his sexual orientation.

Jaguar had obviously mellowed a lot after the whole ordeal. He finally learnt to share the heavy duties in his company with a few of his capable employees. As he delegated more tasks out, he was able to dedicate more time to his wife, his children, and his adorable grandchildren. He also made sure he would see and dine with his parents at least once a week. He'd been taking care of the whole village the major part of his life, so no one would object that it was time for him to devote more time to his immediate family. He had begun to groom his deputy to take on more roles and responsibilities from the village chief. He learnt to let go and entertain the idea that the village was going to do just fine.

***

Jessica walked through the back garden to take the shortcut back to her own house. She was abruptly stopped by Joe, who was hanging out with his mates from the village. There were about five of them sitting around two garden tables with glass tops. There were empty beer bottles and peanut shells all over the table and on the floor.

"Hey sis, we ran out of beer, go and fetch us some more in the fridge."

"Go and fetch your own beer," Jessica responded and took out her packet of cigarettes and lit one up. Within seconds, she heard her mum shuffling footsteps with one arm carrying a bucket filled with ice and beer, while the other held a tray of snacks.

"Your brother is the man of the house now, come help me with these," Helen reminded Jessica.

Reluctantly, Jessica took over the tray and put it down in front of Joe and his friends.

I am just helping mum, she thought to herself, *not serving the new man of the house who did not earn his title nor privilege.*

All the events of the day had given Jessica hope that things had advanced much in the village, and she wondered if she could bring Luke home at the next Chinese New Year.

She watched the smoke from her cigarettes rise up in the air, her brother chatting and laughing with his friends, her mother bringing more food and drinks to them. Through the smoke, she starred at the papaya tree. It's getting crowded on the lowest level with a couple of new baby papaya trees branching out.

Maybe when the papaya tree has grown to resemble a Christmas tree, but not today, not quite yet.

- The End-

ACKNOWLEDGEMENT

My biggest thanks go to Sally Bunker, the renowned botanical artist who is a long-time Hong Kong resident and was supposed to be a retiree who never retires. Sally lives in a beautiful house with a garden landscaped within Mui Wo with her ever-amusing husband, Bob, and her two lovely poodle-Afghan hound mixes. The idea of this book first came to me after the wonderful afternoon spent with Sally and Bob. I was totally in awe by how full of life they both were at their age, and lived life to the full while doing interesting things. I especially found Sally inspiring by how she built her second career and thrived in it at the age of seventy.

The special 'papaya tree' in our village - there was actually such papaya tree and how it gave birth to a new papaya tree out of its trunk never ceased to amaze me. I saw it daily as it was growing along the path that I had to commute to get to the carpark. It never meant much to me except for its weird shape and features, although not anymore. The day I came back from the Bunkers, I looked at this crazy papaya tree in an entirely different perspective. The story was complete after I walked past it and on my way home.

My childhood friend Grace, who's married to an indigenous family, for her kind arrangement for me to interview her father-in-law to get my first-hand sensation of the older generation towards the Government's Small House Policy.

Mr Chan, Grace's father-in-law, who generously gave his time and his views to shed light on a very sensitive topic among the indigenous people.

Frankie Yuen, the man of the people on South Lantau, for his enthusiasm and generous help when I asked him some tricky questions about the laws on the inheritance of Ding rights.

My sister, Katy, who suggested some reference materials to me when I first shared with her my idea of 'Papaya Tree.'

My father-in-law, Ted, who loves cutting down trees; for him to share the motivations, actions, and emotions of his 'hobby.'

My neighbours and friends in the village I live in, for their friendship, kindness, generosity and hospitality. They make the village feel like home for my whole family.

My Editor G, this is the third book we have worked together. Thank you for your impeccable work and always put your heart into my story to make it sparkle.

My husband, Neil, who supports me unconditionally in everything I do and remains my biggest cheerleader in life. My children, Jasmine and Max, for your unlimited love and inspirations for mummy.

About The Author

Papaya Tree is author Orchid Bloom's first novella. Orchid spent her professional life working for luxury brands, most of which within the Travel Retail sector. She lives in Hong Kong with her husband, daughter and son. She loves doing creative works while looking after her family.

www.facebook.com/orchidbloombooks
Orchidbloombooks.com

Also by Orchid Bloom:
Luxe is in the Air
My Roller Coaster Ride to Motherhood

Printed in Great Britain
by Amazon

61518774R00106